The PARTY in ROOM 403 and other stories

The PARTY in ROOM 403 and other stories

Miriam SCHONZEIT

THE JUDAICA PRESS, INC.

The Party in Room 403 and other stories
© 2010 Miriam Schonzeit

ISBN: 978-1-60763-035-7

Editor: Miriam Jakubowicz
Proofreader: Hadassa Goldsmith
Designer: Justine Elliott

THE JUDAICA PRESS, INC.
123 Ditmas Avenue / Brooklyn, NY 11218
718-972-6200 / 800-972-6201
info@judaicapress.com
www.judaicapress.com

Manufactured in the United States of America

CONTENTS

A BIG STEP BACK

"Girls, I need somebody responsible to take care of this project — and somebody with enough initiative and determination to get it done well, as befits an eighth-grade class. Any volunteers?"

The project in question was decorating our eighth-grade classroom in preparation for Rosh Hashanah and Sukkos. It was an especially challenging job this year, since the *Yamim Tovim* fell out so early; Rosh Hashanah was only a week and a half after school started. The girl in charge would have to meet with her classmates to discuss ideas, make a final decision, get money from the teacher to pay for the decorations, buy all the materials, and organize the actual creation and set-up of the new classroom décor.

A daunting job, maybe, on such short notice — for some.

First hand up at Mrs. Waldman's words? Mine, of course.

In fact, mine was the *only* hand up. That didn't bother me at all. In fact, I was used to it.

"Gila?" Mrs. Waldman said. She looked closely at me, almost as if she was sizing me up. I understood why. I'm short with a pixie haircut, and I have what my older sister calls a "delicate look," but first impressions can be misleading. Mrs. Waldman simply hadn't gotten to know me yet. "Are you sure you can handle this?"

"Yes," I said simply. I smiled confidently at the teacher to show her that I meant it. All around me, heads nodded. I saw the respect in many of my classmates' eyes. We'd been together since we were little kids. They all knew me, and they all knew that I could do it.

Mrs. Waldman glanced one more time around the room, then turned to me and nodded. "Okay, Gila, you're on. Do you want me to set up a time for the class to meet and discuss the decorations?"

I shook my head. "No, thank you, Mrs. Waldman. I think we can probably work this out on our own," I answered respectfully. I half turned to face the class. "Okay, everyone?"

Everyone nodded or answered in the affirmative. Mrs. Waldman looked at me again, surprised at the way I'd taken control of the situation so quickly. I smiled sweetly at her. Like I said, she just didn't know me yet. She'd learn about me quickly enough.

The meeting proceeded like a dream. We decided to devote one wall of the classroom to Rosh Hashanah and one to Sukkos. A committee was organized for each wall and then sub-divided into groups of girls to design the decorations, take care of jobs like cutting and gluing, and hang the signs and posters when they were ready.

"Everyone knows exactly what they're doing, right?" I asked at the end of the meeting. Everyone did. The designers were ready to design, the cutters and gluers were ready to cut and glue, and the hangers were ready to hang. Thanks to the positive attitude I'd brought to the meeting, they were all happy to do those jobs, too.

And me? What would be my job? My friend Esther asked me that as we sat on the bus on our way home. "Did you put yourself in any of the groups for the decorations?"

I shook my head. "No. Organizing is a full-time job, Esther. I'll be calling up the heads every night, making sure everything's moving along smoothly, asking Mrs. Waldman any questions that come up — you know, making sure that it all gets done. That's the most important thing, and besides, you know that I'm not a major artist or anything."

Esther nodded. "You sure know how to organize, Gila." Her tone was admiring, but it sounded like there was something less pleasant mixed in as well. Jealousy? Mockery? Either way, it wasn't there as we moved on to the next topic, and I figured that it must have been a product of my overactive imagination.

"Is your family's *sukkah* up yet, Gila?"

I sighed. "I wish! It would be, if I could help with the building—but that's my brothers' job, and they don't get home from yeshivah until after Yom Kippur. My father insists that my job is to help cook and decorate, but I can't decorate it until it's standing!"

"What's the rush?" Esther asked.

I considered the question. "I don't know," I finally answered. "I guess I just like to see things done."

"And done by you." There it was again, that unpleasant note in Esther's voice.

"What's wrong with that?" I asked a bit defensively. After all, Esther knew as well as I did—and certainly as well as my family did—how good I was at organizing. When things were under my control, they got done, and they got done well. Was there something wrong with that?

"Nothing," Esther answered. But something was bothering her—something she didn't like. I could hear it in her voice. She wasn't going to tell me, though. She wanted me to figure it out by myself.

I was really too busy to do that, though. There were a

million and one things to supervise for our class's project. I quickly found myself all but buried in lists and phone calls.

~

"You couldn't get the shiny paper?" I asked Mindy. "Well, why don't you try that new craft store on Elm Street? I'm sure they have it, and if not, let me know. I'll make a few phone calls and make sure we get what we need. The posters will look so much better with the shiny paper—we can't do without it."

"Yup, you're absolutely right, Gila," Mindy answered. "Thanks a million!" She sounded relieved.

I hung up with the feeling of satisfaction that always came from solving the little problems that crop up while working on a project. It felt good, and I was happy with my role—always in the thick of things, moving around, giving orders and getting things done.

The project got done, all right. As usual, it got done well.

By that time, it was nearly Rosh Hashanah, and, with the school project over and done with, I was beginning to get impatient with the slow pace of my family's *sukkah* building.

"Ta, are the boys coming for Rosh Hashanah?" I asked.

"Elchanan is. Dovid is staying in yeshivah for the

Yamim Nora'im this year." My father looked at me curiously. "Why do you ask?" I could understand the question. I loved my brothers and all that, but it was usually my little sisters who couldn't wait for them to come home, not me.

"Oh, I was just thinking that if they were home *motzaei yom tov*, maybe you'd get started on the *sukkah* then. That's all."

My father sighed. "What's the rush, Gilala?" Gilala is his nickname for me. Usually, I like being called Gilala, but right then it just made me more impatient.

"I wanted to get started on the decorating as soon as possible," I answered.

"I want to help," Racheli piped up from her end of the table.

"Me, too," little Miriam echoed.

"Of course you'll help!" I smiled widely at them. And they would, of course. I'd do the directing, the organizing and the bulk of the work, while they'd putter around cutting strings and hanging signs. "And the sooner we can start, the nicer we'll be able to make it."

"Well, you'll have all day *erev* Sukkos — and probably most of the day before," my father told me patiently. "But the boys don't get home until then, so that's when we'll start building. I don't think *motzaei* Rosh Hashanah will give us very much time, since *yom tov* is over so late. And I really could use Dovid's help. It would take much longer to do it with one other person than with two."

"Oh," I said, frowning. I liked to be in the middle of things, getting everything done. It was frustrating to wait for other people to take care of their part of the job, especially when they didn't seem to be as interested in getting the job done as I was.

Luckily for me, there were more opportunities for fun things to take care of in school. On the Monday after Rosh Hashanah, Mrs. Waldman announced yet another project.

"Girls, we're going to have an ongoing *chessed* program in school this year. I have a list of eleven families that need some help after school. Some of these families just had a new baby, and some are large families that could use an extra hand. Your jobs may include taking care of the kids, some light housework or whatever else is needed — probably the same types of things that you'd be doing at home."

I sat up eagerly. This sounded right up my alley. I'd have those houses in tip-top shape, with smiling children and happy parents, in no time at all ….

"Two girls will be assigned to each family. You'll be responsible to go over once a week. Most of you will probably be most needed on Wednesdays or Thursdays so you can help get ready for Shabbos. You can divide the job between you so each of you will go every other week, or you can go together every week. I personally recommend that you go together in pairs since it will probably make the job easier and more enjoyable, but you can do whatever you like. You're eighth graders now, and I trust you to make your own decisions and make sure the job gets done responsibly."

I wasn't sure I liked the idea of working with a partner — I worked best on my own or, better yet, leading a group — but I was sure it would work out in the end. Whoever my partner would be was lucky — really lucky. I was sure that she would realize that, too.

"Now, I need somebody to act as coordinator of the groups. That girl is going to be helping out in a family, too. The job involves keeping track of the girls who are assigned to each family and making sure to let me know if a girl will need to be absent from her *chessed* assignment. Do I have a volunteer?"

Guess whose hand was up first? That's right — mine. It was waving high in the air, and I was proud of it. Here was Gila again, always eager to help out and get the job done.

Mrs. Waldman looked at me, surprised. "Gila, you were in charge of the last classroom assignment, and you did a very nice job, I might add. Are there any other takers?"

The classroom was silent. Everybody looked complacently at me. They were used to me taking charge; they liked it. Most people, I'd discovered over the years, are not natural leaders or organizers. Most people would rather be told what to do and follow directions. My classmates were no exception. They were more than happy to let me take the lead — after all, it meant less work for them.

A slight frown appeared on Mrs. Waldman's face as she scanned the class and then looked back at me. I didn't understand why she was frowning. What was the problem? This was the way our class always did things. I'd volunteer to be in charge, and I'd get the job done admirably. Everyone else would follow along happily and work efficiently under my direction. It was the ideal set-up for everybody, or so I thought.

"Well, okay," Mrs. Waldman finally said after waiting in vain for someone else to raise a hand. "Gila, you've got the job."

I nodded with my usual confidence. "No problem, Mrs. Waldman," I said breezily.

And it wasn't. I helped pair everyone up — ensuring that I was with Esther, of course — and made sure that everyone was happy. I carefully placed the list of partners in a folder in my knapsack, clearly labeling it "*Chessed* Project Partners." I always kept extra folders in my knapsack, just in case a new project came up.

That day was beautiful, just perfect for some outdoor fun.

"Let's play Machanayim," I said as soon as the bell rang for recess.

The classroom rang with eager voices of agreement. "Shira, grab the ball," I instructed the classmate nearest the lockers. "Let's go!"

I left the room, with everybody following right behind me like ducklings behind a mother duck. I didn't realize it until later, but I had been feeling — and behaving — like a mother duck for a very long time, and enjoying it immensely.

I didn't notice that Mrs. Waldman was right behind the last girl out of the room, following all of us — not like a duckling, but like a teacher who smells a problem and wants to find out a bit more. The truth is, even if I had noticed, it wouldn't have made a difference. Life for me was about leading, about being in charge, and I saw nothing wrong with that.

"Teams!" I announced when we got outside. "Sari and Yocheved — you're captains, okay?" They both nodded. They were the best players in the class, and it was only fair to place them on opposite teams. "Sari, your team is Team A, and Yocheved's is Team B. Now let's divide everyone up ...." I walked rapidly among my classmates, assigning everyone an A or a B at random.

"Maybe we should divide up differently this time,"

Bassie said thoughtfully. "We could divide the better players between the two teams. It might be more fair."

I shook my head and moved closer to Bassie. "Girls will feel bad if we do that. It'll be obvious who the better players are if we make up the teams according to skill."

"But it's obvious anyway, and it's frustrating when the teams aren't well matched," Bassie persisted.

I glanced over the teams and saw immediately what she meant. The teams were very uneven. Yocheved's team had most of the good players, while most of the girls on Sari's team could hardly throw a ball. But our old way of dividing teams was more fair, and fair meant good—or so I thought. So I brushed off Bassie with a smile and said, "I don't know. Maybe we should discuss it tomorrow. It's an idea." Then I proceeded to get the game moving. Or rather, I almost proceeded to get the game moving.

I had just announced, "Everybody, move to your places so we can start the game, okay?" when there was a call from the side.

"Gila, can I speak to you for a minute, please?" It was Mrs. Waldman.

I blinked in surprise. I hadn't realized that she was outside with us. I also wasn't used to being singled out by teachers. I almost never misbehaved. Besides, my organization skills usually made their jobs easier.

As I headed over to Mrs. Waldman, my classmates turned to me for instruction.

"Should we wait?" Ariella asked.

"No, just start without me," I ordered. "I'll be there in a minute, as soon as I'm done talking to Mrs. Waldman."

It ended up taking more than a minute. Mrs. Waldman led me under the shadow of a few tall trees that stood near the fence, away from my classmates. Then she turned to face me. She looked serious, almost stern. I was baffled. What had I done wrong?

"I've noticed that you like to be in charge, Gila," Mrs. Waldman said. I nodded hesitantly. The statement was correct, technically, but it bothered me. It wasn't only that I liked to be in charge; it was what I was good at. People *needed* me to be in charge.

"Gila, I want you to think about something. Sometimes, a class has one leader — somebody who organizes, makes decisions and gets things done."

I nodded more confidently. Yes, that was me.

"Sometimes it's a good thing," Mrs. Waldman continued. "But other times, the leader almost …" She frowned, and I knew she was searching for the right words. "… almost takes over, so that the individual feelings and opinions of the classmates don't get expressed."

"But that's not true!" I protested. "Girls can talk about their feelings and opinions. I … we take everyone into account!"

"So what happened before, when Bassie had an idea about dividing up the teams differently? It didn't seem as if she really had a chance to convince the other girls. You managed to work around her, and then you pushed her off."

My head was spinning. That wasn't how it had been — or was it? "B-but I was right! Her way would have embarrassed people!"

"That may or may not be true. Actually, I'm not sure which way would work out better. But that's not my point. My point is that I see the class following your lead all the time — during recess, when working on projects, when making group decisions and formulating ideas. And Gila, that's not healthy. Not for you and not for your classmates."

"Why not?" I asked. I felt numb. It was as if my very identity, the core of my being, was being attacked. I was Gila, the leader, the decision-maker.

"Because other girls may also have leadership abilities, abilities that don't manage to get expressed when you're around because of the very force of your personality. Gila, everyone needs to learn how to lead in certain situations and how to be a follower in others. Nobody can lead *all* the time. And no one can follow all the time, either. Everyone has to know how to stand up for themselves and take control of a situation when necessary. You need to give your classmates that chance, Gila. Your friends can also organize projects, get games moving, come up with ideas. They don't do that because they rely on you to do it for them."

I just stood there, shell-shocked. Mrs. Waldman must have realized how I felt because her tone softened as she told me gently, "It's not easy to change, Gila. But you don't have to change all the way. Your leadership and organizational skills are things that will stand you in very good stead throughout your life. Nobody can take those away from you, and it's the last thing I want to do. All I want is for you to try — just once in a while — to be a follower. Find out how it feels to follow somebody else's lead. Give other girls a chance to take the reins in their own hands."

I stared up at Mrs. Waldman. This may have sounded like a little thing to her, but it was a huge deal to me.

"How?" I asked simply.

Mrs. Waldman smiled. "By taking a step back sometimes; by looking at the whole picture; by keeping quiet when you want to speak up; and letting others take charge. I know that you can find opportunities to do these things, and I know that you will. Gila, you're every bit as much in control of yourself as you are over others — much more, really. No one can ever control other people, and no one can control situations. The only thing that's always in our control is ourselves — how we act, what we do, and what we don't do."

I nodded slowly. Those weren't very clear instructions, but they gave me some idea of what my goals should be. *Taking a step back …*

I was so quiet during the rest of recess and the rest of the day that Esther kept shooting me concerned looks. After lunch, when we decided to play Machanayim again — this time I waited until somebody else suggested it — I approached Bassie.

"I was thinking about your idea, and it sounds like a good one. Why don't you ask the other girls and see what they think?"

Bassie stared at me for a moment. After all, I was Gila. I was always in charge, had all the ideas, made all the decisions and almost never changed my mind. I simply smiled back at her.

We divided up the teams differently. Everybody looked happier, and I realized that other people could have ideas and make decisions, too.

In the afternoon, something else happened to challenge my new goals. Our afternoon teacher, Mrs. Miller, had a project for us, and she wanted someone to be in charge and coordinate the different groups.

I didn't raise my hand. I kept my right hand clenched inside my left and my gaze fixed straight ahead. My classmates eyed me expectantly, and then looked at me with surprise. Only Esther, seated next to me, seemed to have some idea of what I was doing. She gave me an almost imperceptible nod of approval. It was just what I needed to help my hand stay put.

Then Bassie's hand went up. Maybe my earlier encouragement of her idea about splitting the teams had given her new confidence, or maybe her leadership qualities had lain dormant all that time. Mrs. Miller smiled and thanked her for volunteering, and then class moved on. I was the only one who knew that I'd just scored a victory of sorts.

Our *sukkah* was finally up. I carried out the big box of decorations and spread them out on the table with my little sisters.

"Where does this one go, Gila?" Racheli asked, lifting up a large, ornate poster that she'd made the previous year in school.

I opened my mouth to tell her where to hang it, and then I stopped. Who did I think I was? More frighteningly, who did Racheli think I was? After all, I was only two and a half years older than her.

"I don't know, Racheli," I replied, and turned the question around. "Where do *you* think it should go?"

Racheli looked a little surprised at being asked, but she quickly came up with an answer. "Right there," she said, pointing at a spot on the back wall of the *sukkah*, right across from the door.

I couldn't help smiling. That was exactly where I would have put it, but that didn't make it any less of a choice. "Sounds great, Racheli. Do you want to hold it or staple?"

I must admit, I wasn't totally focused on hanging the decorations that year. For one thing, I didn't have to be. I wasn't organizing, ordering and directing. Racheli and Miriam were doing a great job at figuring things out on their own.

For another thing, I had a lot to think about. I was finding out so much about other people, and a lot about myself, too. For some people, moving forward in life means taking a big step forward. For me, it meant something very different. It meant taking a big step back, far enough to see the big picture … and allow *others* to step forward.

FOLLOWING THE TRAIL

"Good morning!" Chumi said brightly. She settled into her desk, right next to her friend Ariella.

"'Morning," Ariella mumbled.

Chumi looked closely at Ariella. Was it her imagination or were her friend's eyes slightly reddened, as if she'd been crying recently? She certainly wasn't imagining anything about Ariella's voice, which was a far cry from her usually cheerful tones.

"Is something the matter?" Chumi asked.

Ariella turned her face away. "No," she said.

Chumi didn't believe her, but she didn't want to press. After all, there were a million and one things that could have upset her friend, most of them relatively minor.

Ariella might be embarrassed about being upset over a petty thing, or she might have a different reason why she didn't want to talk about it. Chumi resolved to mind her own business. She hoped that whatever the problem was, it would blow over on its own.

It didn't.

Chumi reached that conclusion the next morning, when she arrived in school to find Ariella slouched low in her seat. Her face was a mask of doom and her fingers idly doodled meaningless shapes on the front of her History notebook.

Without preamble, Chumi turned to her friend and asked directly, "Ariella, what's wrong?"

"Nothing," Ariella replied. She blew her nose on the damp tissue she was clutching in her right hand. Looking up, she noticed the concern on Chumi's face and added reluctantly, "Well, nothing that I really want to talk about right now, okay?"

Chumi accepted that with a compassionate nod—it was Ariella's right to feel that way—and began to organize her notebooks in preparation for class.

The next day, when Chumi arrived in school to find Ariella staring gloomily out the window, she began to feel a bit impatient. If Ariella was upset about something silly, like any of the small upsetting things that tend to crop up throughout day-to-day life, then she would have cheered up by now. Something bigger was wrong. And what were friends for if not to talk about things that bothered you?

"Ariella," Chumi said, "what's going on? You've looked awful for three days already!"

"Thanks," Ariella said with a watery snort.

"Oh, stop it. You know I didn't mean it like that. But what's the matter?"

Ariella shrugged.

"Come on, maybe I can help."

"You can't. Nobody can. Or at least the people who could help don't care in the least, so what's the point, anyway?"

Chumi frowned. That sounded a little confusing. "But it'll make you feel better to talk things over with someone else."

Ariella just shook her head. "Don't worry. It's nothing major."

"But it must be major if it's been going on for three days already!"

There was no response. Ariella turned back to the window and continued to stare out at the fresh blue sky with eyes that didn't mirror the day's beauty.

Chumi herself felt somewhat downtrodden that day. She was sensitive and kind, and it hurt her to have a friend in trouble. What was most hurtful, though, was the burning need she felt to try and do something to help, when she had no idea what was bothering her friend!

Chumi's cousin and best friend, Sara Hindy, was in

the parallel class in school. Chumi decided to confide in her during lunch. Maybe Sara Hindy would know how to help Ariella.

Slipping into her seat at the lunch table, Chumi opened her sandwich, made a *brachah* and turned to her cousin. "Sara Hindy, I need help."

Sara Hindy rolled her eyes. "Hi, Sara Hindy, how are you? Mind if I eat lunch with you?"

Chumi giggled. "Sorry, it's just that my mind is all twisted in knots! I've been waiting to talk to you all morning. So, uh … hi, Sara Hindy, how are you?"

"*Baruch Hashem*," Sara Hindy replied with an answering grin. "Now what can I do to help you?" she asked in a laughingly pompous tone of voice.

"It's like this. Someone in my class—one of my friends—is upset about something. For three days now she's looked like the world is coming to an end, and she won't tell me what's the matter!"

"Well, she's entitled to keep her problems to herself, isn't she?"

"Sure, but isn't this going a bit too far? I can't help her if I don't know what the problem is! And maybe I *could* help her …."

"So you want to figure out a way to make her tell you?"

"I guess, or else a way to find out on my own, even if she doesn't want to tell me."

"*Hmm* ..." Sara Hindy sat lost in thought for several long moments. Then she shrugged. "I dunno. You'll just have to do some detective work and hope for the best."

"Detective work?"

"Uh-huh. See if you can pick up any clues — things that have been going on in her life, places she's been, people she's been spending time with — and follow the trail. Maybe you'll find out something that will help you."

"Isn't that being nosy?"

"So you'll do it without being nosy! You don't have to start looking through her things and asking questions! Just pay attention to things she does, to what she says ..."

Those seemed like very vague instructions to Chumi, but she didn't have any better ideas. "Okay," she said. "Thanks." The conversation turned to other matters as they finished their lunches.

Chumi was determined to help Ariella. That afternoon, Chumi followed Sara Hindy's instructions and paid close attention to everything Ariella said, every movement she made, anything that might shed light on Ariella's problem.

She picked up a clue completely by accident.

"Okay, girls," Mrs. Aronson said. "I have an interesting assignment for you. It'll be due in three weeks. I'm going to divide up the class into six groups of four. There are twenty-four of you, so that will work out nicely. Now, how to divide you? I'm going to do something a bit different this time and divide you according to birthdays."

"Birthdays?" The girls were surprised. That was an unusual twist to dividing up the class for a school assignment.

"That's right. So, by raise of hand—who was born in January?"

Three hands shot into the air. "Okay, Esther, Shainy and Michal—you're going to start off the first group. Now, let's find the first person born in February. Everyone with a birthday in February, please raise your hands. Now, Nechama Leah, when is your birthday? Okay, Peshy?"

Mrs. Aronson went on, and Chumi found herself tuning out. She couldn't really be blamed, considering that her birthday was the last week of December. Names and dates were called out and swirled around her head as she focused absently on Ariella, wondering …

"All right, we're up to May. Those with May birthdays, please raise your hands …. Okay, Ariella, what date is your birthday?"

Chumi watched Ariella when she answered, "May seventh." At that, Chumi sat up straight in her chair.

"May seventh, *hmm*?" Mrs. Aronson said with a chuckle. "So you had a birthday just two days ago!"

Ariella nodded, and Chumi continued to stare at her,

more confused than ever. If the mystery had been why Ariella was happier than usual, this might have been a wonderful clue. Why was Ariella so sad on the week of her birthday?

The rest of the class went by in a blur. Chumi barely raised her hand in time when Mrs. Aronson asked for the birthdays of those born in December, and earned a frown from her teacher. It hardly registered that she'd just been assigned to work with Shevy, Dafna and Dina Bracha. She couldn't imagine why Ariella was so unhappy, but it seemed too much of a coincidence that her birthday was that week.

Chumi briefly considered confronting Ariella with this information and asking if there was a connection between her birthday and her dismal mood. She discarded the idea quickly, though. Ariella was obviously reluctant to talk about it. If she could possibly help her friend, it would be better to figure out what was going on by herself.

Chumi wasn't sure how to do that, but the answer came to her in a flash when she stepped out of the school building that afternoon and saw Ariella's sister Rochel heading toward the buses.

Rochel was two years younger than Chumi and Ariella. Chumi didn't know her too well; the only times she'd spoken to her was when she'd been at Ariella's house. Chumi was shocked that she hadn't thought to ask Rochel what was wrong. There she was, in the same school, only one floor below her own, the ideal person to know what was happening in Ariella's life—and it had never even dawned on her to speak to her.

Chumi rapidly made up for lost time, though. "Hi, Rochel!" she said brightly, approaching the younger girl as she made her way down to the buses. "Is Ariella's birthday this week?" She didn't want to say anything about Ariella's mood; Ariella might be embarrassed if her sister knew how upset she'd been in school.

Rochel nodded and looked up at her inquiringly. "Her birthday already was, really. It was two days ago."

"That's so nice! Did you do something for her birthday?"

To her surprise, Rochel held up a finger to her lips and looked around nervously. "No, she's not here," Rochel muttered to herself. "My father's been out of town on a business trip," she told Chumi in a hushed voice. "He's coming back tomorrow night, and we're going to make the party then. Ariella doesn't know a thing about it. We wanted to keep it a surprise so we didn't say a word. She probably thinks that we forgot all about her birthday!"

Rochel looked flushed with triumph, but Chumi felt uneasy. Very uneasy. She had a feeling that this was causing Ariella's misery. After all, who wouldn't be miserable if she thought that her family had completely forgotten her birthday?

"Maybe," Chumi suggested quietly, still on the lookout for Ariella, "it would be a good idea to tell her some-thing—even to just give her a hint. Just so that she doesn't keep wondering …."

Rochel shrugged. "But that'll ruin the surprise! Tomorrow, she's going to come home to balloons and streamers and a cake. I can't wait to see the look on her face!"

"But if she thinks that you forgot about her birthday, she'll feel hurt. Isn't it worth it to ruin the surprise so she shouldn't suffer for three days?"

Rochel shrugged again. "Aw, come on, Chumi—you have no idea how hard we've worked on this party! And Ariella's waited for so long. She may as well get a real sur-prise out of it!"

Chumi wasn't sure how much Ariella cared about a real surprise party at that point, but she decided that it wasn't her place to argue.

"Okay," she said simply. "Have a great party tomor-row, then!"

Now that Chumi knew what was bothering Ariella, she had no idea what to do next. Scanning the crowd, she caught sight of Sara Hindy.

"Hey, Sara Hindy!" she called. "Wait up, okay?"

As soon as she caught up to her cousin, Chumi pro-ceeded to explain what she had found out. "I don't know what to do now," she told Sara Hindy. "I can't handle seeing her suffer like this for another day, thinking that her family forgot her birthday! I can just imagine how she feels. I'd feel horrible if I thought my family had forgotten *my* birthday. But the problem is, it's not my secret! I can't tell her; I'd be ruining her family's surprise, and they're obviously working so hard on it."

"Do you think they realize how miserable she is?" Sara Hindy asked.

Chumi shook her head vehemently. "I'm one hundred percent positive that they don't. They would never put her through this if they realized how hurt she was."

"She must be putting on a pretty good show at home, then," Sara Hindy said thoughtfully.

"Yeah, but she isn't at school. I think she's showing her true face here."

"I'm sure," Sara Hindy agreed. "Nobody would pretend to be upset for three days straight—especially not with her friends."

"But what can I do about it?" Chumi asked fretfully. "I feel like I have my hands tied while I'm forced to sit and watch somebody suffer."

There was silence while both girls thought the matter over.

"I have it!" Sara Hindy said suddenly. "Make her your own party! It won't be the same as a family party, but at least it'll be something …."

The next morning, every one of Ariella's classmates carried something extra to school. Most of them hid their bags in their knapsacks—a package of candy, a roll of streamers, a handful of balloons. Others surreptitiously hauled larger objects in shopping bags, like bottles of soda and a big cake with a messy "Happy Birthday, Ariella" written in pink icing.

Chumi supervised everything with a mixture of determination and fear. What if ... what if they somehow made things worse? Nobody knew the story behind the party except for her—and Sara Hindy, of course. She'd only told her classmates that it was for Ariella's birthday. Everyone loves parties, and all the girls were happy to go along with the idea. But how would Ariella feel?

Chumi needn't have worried.

When Ariella walked into the classroom ten minutes into morning recess, after having been detained by Chumi in the hall, her mouth dropped open as she beheld the streamers, balloons and bowls of nosh laid out on the teacher's desk. A large sign hanging across the blackboard proclaimed proudly, "Happy birthday, Ariella!"

To Chumi's relief, Ariella's face broke into a delighted smile. At least somebody had remembered her birthday. Ariella's glance fell on Chumi, and she walked over to her.

"You figured it out," she said simply.

Chumi nodded self-consciously. "Is that okay? Do you mind?"

The wide smile that Ariella gave her told her that she didn't mind — not in the least.

⟋

The best moment of all came that evening, when the ringing of the phone shattered the dinnertime peacefulness in Chumi's house. Leaving her chicken and potatoes half eaten on her plate, Chumi ran for the phone. She had a feeling that she *might* know who was calling … and why.

It was Ariella. "Chumi!" she shrieked into the phone. "Guess what? My family didn't forget my birthday, after all. I'm having another party at home now! It's three days late, but it turns out they planned it this way all along."

"Wow, Ariella, that's amazing!" Chumi said. She felt so happy; this was the way she'd wanted it to be. Ariella was happy, not resentful. She'd been happy even before her second party, because Chumi hadn't wanted her to be upset for another minute.

As soon as Chumi hung up, the phone rang again. This time it was Sara Hindy.

"So? Do you know if her family's party started?" Sara Hindy asked.

"It sure did." The smile in Chumi's voice was obvious. "And Ariella's been the happiest person in the world ever since morning recess — all thanks to you."

"To me?" Sara Hindy echoed.

"Yes, of course! It was all your idea! You told me to make the class party for her, and you were the one who helped me figure out what was bothering her in the first place. You told me to 'follow the trail,' to listen to everything that Ariella said, so I was paying attention when she mentioned her birthday in class. So, of course, it was all because of you!"

"But it wasn't," Sara Hindy said slowly. "Not really. Who noticed that something was wrong, who took the initiative to ask about it, who tried to figure out what the problem could be? Who didn't stop there, but looked to solve the problem once she'd figured it out?"

"Oh, come on," Chumi scoffed. "Anybody would have done that."

"That's not true. Not everyone would — and you were the only one who did."

As Chumi thought about it, she realized that Sara Hindy was right. She wouldn't feel proud and haughty about her accomplishment, but it was good to recognize what she'd done. She'd followed a trail all right, and in the process she'd blazed one of her own — a trail of caring, happiness and friendship.

A SECOND LOOK

When Yosef came by for his weekly visit with his grandfather, he was not in the best of moods. He was glad that it was his day to visit, though, since Zeidy was always ready with a listening ear and a plate of delicious cookies fresh from the bakery.

Sure enough, all Yosef's grandfather had to do was open the door and take one look at his grandson's face before asking, "What's the matter, Yossele?"

"There's this new boy in my class," Yosef said as he sat down on the living room couch. "Most of the kids in my class were with me in elementary school, but some of the ninth graders transferred from other schools for high school—including this boy. We just met, and he's already out to get me! The *rebbi* called on me today when I wasn't paying attention, and this boy started laughing right in my face! And every single time I say something during recess or before class or even during class, he comes up with a reason why I'm wrong. It doesn't matter what we're talking about or what I say. He seems to think that his entire *tafkid* in life is to prove me wrong!"

"Maybe he's jealous?" Yosef's grandfather questioned.

"I don't think so," Yosef responded. "He just doesn't seem like the type, although you never know. I guess I just rub him the wrong way, and boy, does he irritate me! He thinks he's the greatest; he calls out all the answers in class and struts around the school like he's better than everyone else just because he went to such a great elementary school. You can tell he thinks he's a cut above the rest of us, and I don't like it. But none of that would matter; I'd just leave him alone and he'd leave me alone, except that he doesn't want to do that. For some reason, he's decided to single me out as his enemy."

"Maybe he senses the way you feel about him?" Yosef's grandfather suggested.

Yosef shook his head back and forth vehemently. "How would he know? I'm telling you, he's the type of kid who just likes to make trouble. He decided that I'm the one he's going to bother, and I just have to suffer until he gets bored of me and picks on somebody else."

As usual, Zeidy was a good listener. He said very little and let Yosef talk for as long as he wanted. It wasn't until Yosef was getting ready to leave that he realized he hadn't asked his grandfather how he was doing.

"Zeidy," he said, "I'm sorry. I've been so busy complaining, I forgot to ask how you're feeling."

"*Baruch Hashem*," his grandfather smiled. "No better, but at least no worse."

"And is your friend Moishele still coming?" Moishele was a boy who lived on the block and had lately taken to visiting and helping Yosef's grandfather.

Zeidy's eyes lit up. "Oh, yes! He's growing up, too. Such a fine young man. A real *baal chessed*. He comes over with a package of his mother's cookies and asks if I need anything."

"Do you really think he's my age, Zeidy?"

"I think so. He mentioned this week that he just started high school, so he should be your age."

"Do you know what school he goes to, Zeidy?" Yosef asked.

His grandfather shook his head as a thoughtful look suddenly came over his face. "I'm not sure," he answered vaguely. "You had better head home for supper, Yossele. Have a good week. Thank your mother again for letting you come."

A few minutes after the door closed behind Yosef, the bell rang again.

"Moishele!" beamed Mr. Kagan as he opened the door to behold his second guest that afternoon. "What brings you here on a Thursday? I usually only have the honor of your presence on Mondays."

Moishy's downcast face was his answer. "I came to talk," he said. "Can I come in?"

"Of course," said Mr. Kagan, escorting his visitor inside and seating him on the couch. "What's the matter?"

"School is awful. Just plain awful. I hardly know anyone, and there's this one boy who's just impossible. He's a class leader and he loves to boss everyone around, and the funny thing is that the other guys seem to put up with it most of the time. But yesterday, he started bossing *me*—and I showed him what I'm made of! I refused to allow myself to be ordered around, and now he's out to get me."

"Are you sure he's really out to get you?" Yosef's grandfather asked. "Maybe you're just extra sensitive because you're new in school?"

"No," Moishy answered. "He really doesn't like me. I can tell. He's always one of the captains of our class's teams by recess—and somehow, I always get chosen last. Never third to last, or second to last, but *last*! This has been going on for a few days already, and I'm as good at a game of ball as most of the class is. And he's such a clown, Mr. Kagan! He's always coming up with silly comments during class—and half the time, the teachers actually laugh!"

"A real class leader, *hmm*?"

"I guess so. The type that can do whatever he wants, be mean whenever he feels like it and still have everyone think that he's terrific." Moishy's tone was bitter—as bitter as Yosef had sounded just half an hour ago, Mr. Kagan realized.

Something was bothering him, something about the way Moishy had described the boy—a leader, with a lively sense of humor. And of course, it was a small yeshivah.

"Tell me, Moishele," Mr. Kagan said. "What's this boy's first name?"

Moishy looked surprised, but he imagined that a first name wouldn't be *lashon hara*. After all, Mr. Kagan didn't go to his yeshivah and didn't know anything about his class.

"His name is Yosef," he answered his elderly friend.

Moishy didn't understand why Mr. Kagan heaved a huge sigh at that remark, but he did know that he felt better after talking to somebody. He spoke to his elderly friend for a few more minutes and asked how he was feeling, and then it was time to go.

"Bye, Mr. Kagan. I'll see you on Monday, okay?"

"Okay, Moishele. Tell me, did you happen to bump into anyone going down the stairs outside as you came up?"

"No, but there are two sets of stairs. If someone else was leaving, he might have gone down the other staircase, and we would have missed each other. Why?"

Mr. Kagan just shook his head. "Oh, just wondering." With a thoughtful expression on his face, Mr. Kagan watched as Moishy headed toward the stairwell.

The next week, Yosef arrived at his grandfather's apartment right on time. He had only knocked on the door one time when it swung open. His grandfather stood in front of him, beaming.

"Come in, Yossele," he said. "There's somebody here I want you to meet. You know how you keep asking about Moishele?"

Yosef's heart jumped. "Moishele? He's here?"

"He sure is," his grandfather answered. "Come into the living room and have a look."

Yosef rounded the corner and walked into the living room. He stared hard. Were his eyes deceiving him?

Moishy was seated on the couch and looked just as astonished as Yosef. He picked up the cup that was sitting on the coffee table in front of him and began to play with it. Both boys finished examining each other without a sound and then stared at Yosef's grandfather accusingly. It was clear that they felt betrayed.

Yosef's grandfather smiled gently as he pointed to the couch. "Come sit down, Yosef."

Yosef had a stubborn look on his face and his arms were crossed over his chest. He dragged his feet against the carpet as he obeyed his grandfather, clearly unhappy to do so.

"I'm going to the kitchen to get some more cookies and a bottle of soda," his grandfather said. He seemed completely unperturbed by the murderous looks both boys were shooting each other.

Yosef and Moishy remained in the room. Yosef looked up toward the ceiling, out the window, at the plants spread across the low table on the far side of the room to catch the sunlight — anywhere but at Moishy, his worst enemy. Moishy looked stubbornly down at his sneakers.

It seemed to take Yosef's grandfather an inordinate amount of time to return from the kitchen. When he did, he placed a bottle of soda and three plastic cups on the table.

"*Oy, vey!*" he said. "I forgot the cookies!" He headed back into the kitchen.

Yosef felt his curiosity beginning to overcome his anger and resentment. He wanted to ask, to find out, to understand what was going on, but he angrily pushed back those urges. This wasn't right; it wasn't *fair*! What was his biggest enemy doing seated comfortably on his grandfather's couch, right where Yosef usually sat? He sealed his lips tightly and focused on the topmost branches of a tree planted right outside the large picture window.

Moishy gave into his curiosity first. "Mr. Kagan is *your* grandfather?" His voice expressed disbelief.

Yosef nodded curtly.

"Mr. Kagan told me that he had a grandson named Yossele, but I never thought it was *you*." The implied criticism came through loud and clear, but Yosef still felt compelled to ask his own question.

"You're the Moishele who comes to visit every week?"

Now it was Moishy's turn to nod.

The room was quiet except for the ticking of the big clock in the corner. A million conflicting thoughts seemed to run through Yosef's head all at once. Zeidy had spoken so highly of Moishele! Moishele was the one who carried in the groceries, who came over to walk Zeidy to shul for Minchah, who brought over cookies and soup and laughter. When Zeidy had spoken about Moishele, he sounded so good as to be almost … unreal. Too good to be true.

How could this wonderful Moishele be the same Moishy Gruner who taunted him at every opportunity, who was his sworn enemy at recess and who did whatever he could to best Yosef at everything? It just didn't make sense.

Yosef happened to glance up just then and caught sight of Moishy's face. Moishy looked as shocked as Yosef felt. Suddenly, Yosef saw things from Moishy's point of view.

Moishy was probably wondering how Yosef's grandfather had a grandson who was so ... argumentative, bossy, such a troublemaker in school.

Another thought popped into Yosef's head. If Moishy was so good to his grandfather, it was impossible — simply impossible! — that he was every bit as bad as Yosef had thought.

Two very thoughtful boys sat in the living room when Yosef's grandfather finally came back with a tray of cookies. His eyes were twinkling, but neither boy thought to wonder why it had taken so long to bring in the small platter.

"So, Moishele and Yossele, how are you enjoying each other's company in school?"

Once again, the room became so quiet that the only sound was the steady ticking of the clock in the corner.

"I dunno," said Moishy, rubbing the toe of his shoe against the leg of the coffee table.

Yosef shrugged.

"Both of you are such special, special boys," said Yosef's grandfather, looking directly at each of them in turn. They squirmed slightly. Yosef's grandfather was silent for a long minute, and then he spoke again.

"I'm a little tired today, boys. I could use a few things from the grocery store down the block. How about if you go together to pick them up while I take a short nap?"

What could they do? How could they say no? The

two boys quietly stood up, accepted the shopping list, said separate good-byes to Yosef's grandfather and left the apartment.

Yosef's mind was spinning. It might have been nice to get out of the apartment and be able to think a little — but not while he was walking next to Moishy Gruner! Moishy, walking alongside him, seemed to feel the same way. His head was held high and his lips were sealed tight. His every mannerism bespoke the fact that he might have been forced to go somewhere with Yosef, but that didn't mean he had to enjoy it!

When they entered the store, Yosef unfolded the list his grandfather had handed him. His frown deepened.

Moishy, watching, couldn't help asking, "What's the matter?"

Yosef simply handed over the list. Soon Moishy's face mirrored his own. It was the most vague shopping list either boy had ever seen. The first item was "pasta."

"I guess we should get one box of macaroni," Moishy muttered. "That's probably the most popular kind of pasta."

Neither boy was sure, though. The next item on the list was "berries."

"Fresh or frozen?" Yosef mumbled.

"And what kind of berry?" Moishy spoke slowly, as if he was trying to figure something out. "What's going on here? Your grandfather's lists are always so clear."

Yosef had already realized what was going on, and he shared his knowledge unwillingly.

"My grandfather wants us to talk to each other," he said. "I don't think he really cares what we buy."

Moishy nodded, and a smile began to tug at the corners of his mouth. "Well, it's working. In that case, why get macaroni? Let's get that funny squiggly pasta with three colors!"

Yosef paused for a long minute. Making a scavenger hunt out of his grandfather's list sounded fun, and he couldn't help but agree to the idea. "All right," he found himself saying. "And I've got an idea for 'berries.'"

The two boys did have fun. They bought frozen raspberries for "berries," ice cream for "dairy products" and a can of anchovy fillets for "fish." By the time the cart was packed up into two large bags for each of them to carry, they were laughing together like two old friends.

Yosef's grandfather was not surprised by the unusual groceries or the two cheerful faces.

"I have a question for you," he said, as he helped the boys unpack the interesting food items into the pantry and refrigerator. "Let's say I would have given this list to each of you and sent you off to the store independently. Would you have brought home the same items?"

Both boys shook their heads no.

"Why not?"

"Because the things you wrote down were too vague,"

Yosef answered immediately. "So many different types of food could fit under the items that you wrote down."

"We could buy different things for fish, for dairy products, for berries ... whatever we thought you meant," Moishy contributed. Both Yosef and his grandfather couldn't help noticing that this time, Moishy had actually agreed with his rival. They were having a discussion without a single argument or angry word.

"That's right," Yosef's grandfather stated. "Two different people can read from the same list and arrive at two completely different conclusions. It all depends on how you see things. It's the same thing when you look at another person. One person can see someone else and focus on the good and the beauty, while another person will see only the bad. Once you get stuck in that kind of rut, it's very hard to start seeing the good again."

Yosef's grandfather looked directly at both boys. "I think you've both gotten off to a good start at seeing some positive things about each other, *hmm*?"

Yosef looked at Moishy, and Moishy looked at Yosef. They both thought about the other's relationship with the same wonderful person, about the fun they'd just had shopping together. They both realized that there was plenty more good that had yet to be discovered. Maybe they just needed to take a second look.

BEST LEFT UNSAID

"The test on the whole Civil War unit will take place a week from today," Mrs. Klein announced crisply.

There was a chorus of groans. Mine was one of the loudest. I didn't hate history, I didn't hate tests and I certainly didn't hate studying—not with friends, bowls of popcorn and plenty of good cheer to go around—but it was the thing to do.

"Girls!" Mrs. Klein eyed us sternly. "This is a short unit, and I'm giving you plenty of time to study. We've covered this unit well, and I think all it will take is a night or two of good studying and you'll all do just fine. Now, please open your books to page 306."

I opened my book to the required page and wrote the

date on the top of a fresh piece of loose-leaf paper in fancy, curly lettering. Mrs. Klein had written one underlined word — *Reconstruction* — on the blackboard, so I copied that down in the center of my paper in big, curly letters as well. Then, as Mrs. Klein began to talk, I surreptitiously pulled a pink paper off my pad of post-it notes and jotted down a note for my friend Riva. *Study at my house Sunday night?* I wrote on it. *Love, Bashie.*

Of course, I knew Riva would study with me — and Sharona and Frumie and Malky. And maybe Chaya and Gila, if they were interested. I always studied in a group. Sharona liked to teach and the rest of us liked to listen. And we all liked the nosh and schmoozing and plain old fun we always had at our studying parties. My mother was fine with this so long as I came home with decent grades and had time for a good night's sleep — both of which I accomplished without too much difficulty, most of the time.

I folded up the note, wrote a big *R.* on the outside of the paper, and passed it to Esty, who was sitting next to me, so she could pass it to Gila, and then Gila could pass it to Riva.

But no note came back.

I had to spend the rest of the lesson listening halfheartedly and jotting down real notes as Mrs. Klein explained all about the rebuilding of the Southern states after the Civil War.

The lack of a return note wasn't so surprising, though. Riva might have gotten nervous; her seat was more in Mrs. Klein's line of vision than mine was. Or one of the girls between us may have refused to serve as messenger. That had happened plenty of times, too.

It was during recess time that I got my big surprise.

Riva strolled up to me, proffering a bag of corn chips. "Hey, Bashie, how about studying at my house on Sunday for the test next week?"

I blinked. "Okay. Or we could do it at my house; I don't care. Didn't you get my note?"

"Nope," she said. "Did you talk to Frumie yet?"

"No, I didn't talk to anyone." I wondered who had botched up the sending of the note. Had Esty finally refused to pass it on? I knew that she objected pretty strongly to note-sending, but usually she'd offer some warning if she really planned on leaving it folded up on the corner of her desk. Today she'd accepted it without a whisper or shake of her head, even if she *had* frowned.

Well, maybe Gila had dropped it and was afraid to pick it up, or maybe one of them had been waiting for Mrs. Klein to turn her back, and then forgotten to pass it on. It really didn't matter. I pushed the note out of my head.

That was when I felt—before I heard or saw—that someone else was standing next to me. I turned ... and came face to face with Rivky Perlstein.

I was surprised to see her standing beside me. Rivky had joined our class at the beginning of the year, and she seemed to, well ... blend in with the woodwork. For maybe a week or two, she'd remained a new face, a novelty, somebody to be nice to, and then everyone just kind of forgot about her. I'm in a nice class with good girls, but when somebody blends in so well with the desks and chairs, it's hard to remember that she's there.

"Hi, Rivky," I said, smiling. "What's up?"

She held out a tightly clutched pink sticky note. *My note.* What was Rivky doing with it? Almost instantly, I realized that it didn't really matter. What mattered was the fact that Rivky had it now, and that she obviously thought she was the intended recipient. I stared down at the note dumbly, reading my invitation — meant for Riva — to come study at my house on Sunday.

"Thanks for the note," she said in a nervous voice. "I ... that sounds nice."

I had no idea what to say or what to do. Should I tell Rivky that the whole thing was one big mistake? Should I act like I had really sent her the note and tell her I was looking forward to her coming? But I was already studying with a whole group!

Rivky must have seen the parade of thoughts reflected on my face. Anxiously, she said, "*Was* the note meant for me? It just said *R.* on it, but it came to my desk, so I thought ..."

I looked at her then — really looked at her — and I couldn't help seeing that her eyes were filled with a mixture of worry and hope. Rivky desperately wanted me to agree, to tell her that of course the note was for her.

So I did. I managed a big smile back, and said, "Of course it was for you! So are you going to be able to come?"

Rivky's face was flooded with relief. "Yes," she said happily. "Unless you want to come to my house? It doesn't matter to me, and my mother likes me to bring home friends."

"Uh, maybe my house would be better, this time. I … uh, I sometimes study with Riva and some other girls. Do you mind if they come over, too?"

Rivky looked a little apprehensive, but she shook her head. "No. That's fine."

"Okay, great. I'll call you Sunday morning, then." I smiled at Rivky and watched her face light up again. "D'you know what time will be good for you?"

Rivky shrugged. "It doesn't matter. Any time is fine." She spoke with an eagerness that made me uncomfortable. Rivky was so excited — and I hadn't even invited her, really.

Should I say something? The question plagued me throughout the afternoon. It felt as if I was lying both to myself and to Rivky. She wouldn't have to feel stupid if I told her the truth. It wasn't her fault that somebody had passed my note to the wrong *R*.

No, it was too late. Maybe if I'd looked at her blankly when she first came over to me, I could have done something, but I'd already told her that the note was from me. Now I was stuck in the lie. Was it really a lie, though? And if it was, it couldn't be wrong not to correct my mistake, right? After all, it would only hurt Rivky's feelings. There are some things that are just better left unsaid.

But what about you? a little voice bubbled up angrily. *You don't want to study with Rivky. She's not your type. She won't be any fun. You'll spend three hours just studying, with nobody knowing what to say to Rivky. Maybe no one else will even want to study with you anymore once they find out that Rivky's coming. Who knows if she even knows the material well? You didn't do anything wrong. You sent a note that was obviously for Riva and it got sent to Rivky instead. That's not your fault. And if you don't want to study with Rivky, you'd better correct this mistake before it gets even bigger. Who knows where this could lead?*

I almost wanted to listen to that little voice, but the other side of me — the compassionate, caring side that thought about other people and doing the right thing almost as much as my little-voice-side thought about having fun — told me that I just couldn't do it. Rivky *would* be embarrassed. She *would* feel stupid. It wouldn't matter that the note came to her by mistake. She'd still feel dumb — on top of feeling disappointed and let down. Here she was, finally looking forward to studying with other girls, making new friends ….

Why can't she make friends in school, or invite girls over to study at her house? It was the mean little voice again. *Friendship isn't a one-way street, you know. What does she think she's doing, sitting back and just waiting for friendship to pile into her lap?*

The better part of me whispered back that she was just shy. That I couldn't understand how Rivky felt, because I myself wasn't shy. That I wasn't committing myself to anything besides for studying with somebody else for a few hours. There didn't have to be a best-friendship, Shabbos invitations and school projects together; there didn't even have to be another studying session together, if I didn't want one.

What mattered right now was that I didn't shame Rivky, that I made sure she never found out the truth about the note. Because there were some things that shouldn't be said.

My friends were surprised—but not unpleasantly so—when I awkwardly told them that I'd agreed to study with Rivky for the test.

"That's a great idea, actually," Sharona said. "We should have thought of it earlier. She seems so shy. It's a great way to get to know her better."

The others agreed.

"That's so cute you thought of it, Bashie," Malky said.

"Cute?" I asked. "Why?"

"Oh, it's just, well … I don't know. Not your type," Malky answered.

I felt just a little taken aback. What did she mean, it wasn't my type? Because I wasn't friendly? Because I didn't think about other people? And the most uncomfortable part was that Malky was right. It wasn't exactly something I'd "thought of" at all. The whole thing had just tumbled into my lap—and I'd almost tried to push it right out again.

I had a lot to think about as I walked home from school that afternoon.

I had even more to think about after our Sunday study session. It had gone well. Rivky was certainly smart—every bit as smart as Sharona. Everybody had enjoyed her company, and I had the feeling that she'd enjoyed ours, too.

The question was, now what? What should I do about the next test, which would be taking place in less than a week?

My friends answered that question for me.

"You'll ask Rivky to study with us again, right?" Riva asked at lunch.

"Why not?" I answered. "As long as you're all okay with it."

Everyone was more than okay with it. It was good we'd settled that, because just then Rivky walked into the lunchroom and sat down next to me, a sweet smile on her face.

"Rivky, you'll study with us for the *Navi* test, too, right?"

Another smile. Rivky had two dimples that showed when she smiled. "I'd love to. Thanks," she said.

And it continued. Not just for the *Navi* test, but for the next Science test and then our *Halachah* test and our *Chumash* midterm. And sometime in between, she'd invited me to come over on Shabbos afternoon, and I felt that I couldn't say no. Then I had to invite her to come over to my house the following Shabbos. She joined my group for our Current Events project, and even invited me to come to the mall with her family on Sunday.

It was as if we were becoming fast friends. Only it was all on her end.

I was the first to admit that Rivky was a really, really nice girl. She was smart and sweet and could even be funny and friendly when you got to know her. But she was still quiet and shy, and I couldn't help being bored around her sometimes. She had a nervous giggle that meant she was somewhat ill-at-ease, and she had a terrible habit of biting her nails. I couldn't get used to those things—or I didn't want to.

Rivky's presence was becoming a drag. She sat with me during lunchtime every day. My friends were there, too, and everyone was friendly to her, but if there was an empty seat next to me, that was the one she always chose. During recess, she played whatever I played. Every time a class project was announced, she'd crane her neck and look over at me with hopeful eyes. What could I do? Say no?

It wouldn't have been so bad if she'd had another friend. But I felt like she was always turning to me — for every test, every project, every game. And I was beginning to feel stifled.

Every year, the eighth grade ran our school's Purim carnival. They were in charge of the booths, handed out refreshments and changed the CD in the portable stereo system. This year, it was finally our turn to be in charge!

When the principal came into our classroom to talk to us about the carnival, it was all we could do to sit in our seats and listen patiently as she detailed the plans and rules and program. Then it was time to divide ourselves into small groups and sign up to run the booths.

I looked over at Riva and opened my mouth — and then Rivky was there, too, looking at me expectantly. All at once, I didn't want to be with Rivky again. I couldn't.

It was just too much. But Riva had already noticed Rivky and was smiling a welcoming smile.

"We'll all be together," Riva said brightly.

Rivky beamed, and I smiled stiffly. That was it, then. I was stuck—as usual.

I got home late that afternoon, since I walked home slowly, and I noticed my mother watching me as I ate supper. I must have had a pretty long face. When we ended up in the kitchen after supper, just the two of us, she asked me what was wrong.

My mother was washing the dishes, and before I started to talk, I picked up the dish towel and began drying the plates. It was a good way to let off my frustration. I rubbed the dishes until they were all dry and shiny. As I dried, I talked, and my mother listened.

"And what's the worst that could happen now?" my mother asked slowly, when I finished telling over the story.

"What's the worst? Oh, I don't know …. I'll have to go on being friends with her forever, I guess."

"And is that so terrible? What I mean to say is, it's not keeping you from spending time with your other friends, right? And she isn't exactly bothering you, is she?"

"No, she's not," I had to agree. But still … "Ma, I don't want to always have to hang out with her and study with her. Now she *expects* us to do lots of things together and … I don't want to." I said the last part in a small voice, embarrassed. Even to my own ears, my problem sounded almost selfish, and definitely petty.

"I hear." My mother was quiet for a long minute. "So what it boils down to is this: You can give her the cold shoulder and let her figure out that the friendship is over, or you can go on spending some of your time being nice to her and doing things with her that you enjoy, even if you'd prefer to do them by yourself or with a different friend."

I squirmed. "But Ma, it's really not as bad as it sounds …"

"Are you sure, Bashie? You did tell me that she doesn't have any other friends. What will she do if you drop her? And is the time you spend with her really so bad?"

There was a long silence. No, Rivky really didn't have any other friends—not yet, anyway. And no, the time I spent with her wasn't all that bad. A little boring, maybe. But was it worse than that? Not really.

I looked at my mother. She didn't look judgmental or upset at me. In fact, she was smiling with understanding—and I knew, right then, that my mother had no question about what I was going to do. She knew—absolutely, positively knew—that I was going to do the right thing.

All that was left for me to do, then, was to do it.

It wasn't easy. But … it wasn't terribly hard either, or terribly anything. Rivky *was* a nice girl. She was certainly smart, even if I wasn't really the type to appreciate her analytical mind. And she had a sense of humor, even if it wasn't perfectly in line with my own. In fact, I was almost used to having Rivky at my side, going places with me and my friends, accompanying me to study sessions … when it all ended.

Nava came into our class in the middle of the year. She was soft-spoken and smart, with sparkling blue eyes and a smile that lit up the room. She and Rivky were drawn to each other like magnets. I could see them talking to each other at recess, sitting next to each other at lunch and sharing jokes on the bus. It was the funniest thing, but I wasn't sure how I felt about that. I almost missed having Rivky slide in next to me, with her shy smile and gentle comments.

"Are you coming to my house tomorrow to study for the history test?" I asked Rivky about a week after Nava entered our class.

Rivky clapped a hand to her forehead. "Oh, no! I'm so sorry, Bashie. I meant to call you last night and tell you. I was going to study with Nava this time. I figured you'd have the rest of the group to study with, but I wanted to check with you and let you know. Is that okay?"

"Sure, no problem," I answered. I meant it, but I wasn't as happy as I'd thought I'd be. I almost thought

I'd miss her sitting in the corner, bent over her notes covered with her neat, even handwriting, her long ponytail brushing the paper as she read a paragraph out loud or clarified a point.

And I did miss her. In fact, I had a feeling that I missed Rivky more than she missed me! But there was no denying it: Rivky was happier now with Nava than she'd been with me. They were more suited to each other. Rivky and I had never been cut out to be close, but the friendship had been good for both of us. For Rivky—because she hadn't had a choice. A person needed a friend. And for me—because it had taught me a lesson.

I'd learned that I could be friends with somebody who was different from me. I could give up my time and attention for other people, and have fun in the bargain. I'd come to realize that there are situations and places and friendships that may not seem ideal, but they can still be pretty good!

Of course, Rivky and I stayed friends, in a casual sort of way. We'd talk for a few minutes before class and even work together on a project here and there.

And no, I never told anybody—never. Rivky never knew why we'd studied together for that test way back at the beginning of eighth grade. My friends never knew why I'd studied with Rivky, or why we'd continued to be friends.

It was a secret between my mother and me. Because, after all, there are some things that are just better left unsaid.

THE PARTY IN ROOM 403

Yoni was right there, sitting up in the hospital bed amid white sheets, white blankets and white pillows while his parents conferred with the doctor. He clenched the bottom of his striped hospital pajama top so tightly that his knuckles ached.

"It's his cousin," Yoni's mother said emotionally, "and his best friend."

"And Yoni seems so much better already," his father added. "He doesn't have to be there for the whole thing. We can just take him for an hour or two and then bring him home — or back to the hospital for another night if you still want to keep an eye on him."

The doctor heard them out. One thing Yoni had grown to appreciate about Dr. Wilson over the past three days was the fact that he was deliberate, patient and thoughtful—unlike some other doctors Yoni and his family had experienced the dubious pleasure of meeting.

Now, though, Yoni felt impatient. Couldn't the doctor just give an answer already? When his parents finished speaking, he held his breath. The doctor just stood there, fingers interlocked and head bowed contemplatively. A couple of seconds ticked by and Yoni was forced to let out his breath with a *whoosh* that made him ache all over. He leaned back against the pillows, gasping. Maybe it hadn't been a good idea to try and hold his breath while he was still feeling sick.

Finally, the doctor opened his mouth. To Yoni, he looked like a bespectacled, white-robed judge about to pass down a verdict. "I don't think it's a good idea. It would be irresponsible of me to encourage it. Yoni still needs hospital care at this time—and that's not going to change by tonight. He definitely does look better, and he should. But he's still recovering from relatively serious surgery, and it's not the time for him to attend parties, no matter how special or important they may be." He half-turned toward Yoni. "I'm sorry. I see that this means a lot to you, but your health comes first."

Yoni's parents nodded solemnly. The doctor was right. Yoni's health did come first, of course.

Yoni couldn't bring himself to agree, although he knew that he couldn't argue with the doctor's logic. In fact, when he opened his mouth, he found that he couldn't say anything. There was a golf-ball-sized lump in his throat, and it was hard enough to get air past it in order to breathe—never mind speak.

He couldn't believe it. Of all the weeks to end up in the hospital with appendicitis, why'd it have to be this one? He'd been looking forward to Moshe's *bar mitzvah* for so long. Like his mother had told the doctor, they were both cousins and best friends.

Yoni could almost picture the hall being set up right now for the momentous event that would be taking place that evening. He knew all the details about the menu and the centerpieces, and which photographer they were going to use. He even knew Moshe's speech almost by heart. Was it just this past Shabbos when they'd joked about it? Moshe had said that Yoni could fill in for him if he got stage fright, but it seemed as if that wouldn't be an option anymore ….

The doctor left the room, his rubber-soled shoes padding softly on the white linoleum floor. They were white, to match the doctor's long white coat. Everything was white. Yoni hated the hospital. Right now, it felt like a white prison.

His parents came to stand by his bed. Yoni smiled up at them shakily.

"I'm sorry you won't be able to make the *bar mitzvah*," his father said gently.

His mother had tears in her eyes. "We tried, Yoni."

Yoni nodded. "I know," he said. He was upset at himself for allowing his voice to shake. He tried to control it when he said, "Don't worry, I'll be fine," but it sounded even worse.

"I'll be back tonight to stay with you," his mother told him.

Yoni managed to object to this. After all, Tante Malka was his mother's sister, and he knew that she'd been looking forward to this celebration nearly as much as he had. "No, Ma, don't. Really, I'll be fine here. The doctor said I still need to rest, so I'll just rest. Don't leave the *bar mitzvah*, okay?"

His mother hesitated. "Are you sure?"

Yoni nodded, and even managed to plaster a smile on his face. For several more minutes before they left, he continued to reassure his parents that he was fine.

When he was alone, Yoni pulled the covers up to his chin and gave in to the tears that had been threatening to overflow since the doctor's verdict. He may have been almost *bar mitzvah* himself, but that didn't keep the disappointment from being as painful as any physical hurt he'd felt over the past few days—even the terrible pain in his stomach that had brought him to the hospital in the first place.

With the blankets nearly covering his face and the door to the room halfway closed, Yoni cried.

Yoni woke up to find the sun sending slanted rays of light into his room. That was strange; he must have drifted off. It seemed to be late in the afternoon. A quick glance at his watch confirmed that it was six o'clock. Moshe's celebration would be starting soon — and Yoni would not be there.

The phone rang, startling Yoni. He hesitated for a moment, not really wanting to speak to anyone just then. After two rings, his curiosity overcame his unwillingness, and he picked up the receiver.

"Hello?"

"Hey, Yoni! It's Moshe!"

"Hi!"

"I just wanted to tell you that I'll be missing you tonight — a lot! What am I gonna do when I forget my speech?"

Yoni couldn't help grinning at the comic dismay in Moshe's voice. "You'll manage, I'm sure. You won't even realize that I'm not there."

"That's not true!" his cousin protested. "I'll be thinking about you every second. I really wanted to come to the hospital now and see you for a couple of minutes before the *bar mitzvah*, but we kind of ran out of time."

"That's all right," Yoni found himself reassuring someone for what seemed to be the millionth time that evening. "I'm fine, but I'll be thinking about the *bar mitzvah* the whole night."

"I'll save you a piece of cake."

"Good. Make it a big one," Yoni replied, even though the thought still made him feel a little sick to his stomach.

"You should see what's going on here now. Michal had her hair done and the clip just fell out and she's going bananas. I wish you could be here to—" Moshe's voice broke off and Yoni heard him yell, "What? Oh, okay."

He got back on. "Sorry, Yoni. I hafta go. My father wants to talk to me for a couple of minutes before we leave for the hall—hairclip or no hairclip, I guess. So I'll be seeing you when you get out tomorrow, huh?"

"I guess so. Anyway, it sounds like you better go. *Mazel tov.*"

"Thanks!" Moshe answered. "Have a *refuah sheleimah.*"

"Thank you! And Moshe? Thanks for calling, okay?"

The lines clicked. Once more, Yoni was left to his own devices. He remembered that he had to *daven* Minchah and began davening, stretching it out for a full ten minutes. Then he was again left wondering what to do. Yoni had books and even a couple of borrowed electronic games sitting on the night table, but he was unable to summon the interest to look at them. All he could think about was the *bar mitzvah*.

Moshe was for sure in the van already, surrounded by his whole family. Yoni's family was probably on the way by now, too. Only Yoni was stuck all by himself in a hospital bed ....

Restlessly, Yoni stood up. It was going to be an awful, boring night; he was sure of it. How could it be otherwise when he was trapped in the hospital on the night of his cousin's *bar mitzvah*? Still, he didn't have to spend all of it lying in bed.

Still a little shaky on his feet, Yoni paused as he stood next to the bed. He held tightly to the railing for a few seconds to make sure he had his balance before moving away. All he was attached to now was his IV pole, and that would travel with him just fine. Until now, he'd only walked the distance to the bathroom and the window at the far end of the room. Now he felt like going a bit further.

He slowly left the room and made a left, heading down the hall. There was a nearby recreation room where he'd spotted some other kids playing when he'd been wheeled past it yesterday. Yoni thought that it would be nice to see some other kids and check out some new games. Maybe that would distract him.

Yoni was halfway to the recreation room. He was almost happy to see that the short walk wasn't tiring him at all. Nothing, though, he assured himself dismally, would make him *totally* happy right then.

He looked up for a moment to gauge his progress and suddenly found himself staring at a bright bouquet of balloons standing at the entrance to the next hospital room — Room 403, he noticed. He had balloons in his room, too, but these looked different somehow. He realized why instantly.

Not one balloon said "Get Well" or "Thinking of You," or was decorated with hearts or flowers. Instead, the balloons in this bouquet were bright and said "Congratulations" and — Yoni blinked to make sure he wasn't seeing things — "*Mazel tov!*"

What was a *mazel tov* balloon doing in a hospital? It seemed so out of place.

Yoni was not the type of boy to knock on hospital doors when he didn't know the patients inside, but, driven by a mixture of boredom and curiosity, he found himself tentatively tapping on the open door.

"Come in," a voice said.

Yoni went in. He found himself face to face with a boy who seemed to be about his age. Like Yoni, he was wearing a *yarmulke*. He also looked like he'd just finished a recent bout of crying, and he appeared to be bored and unhappy.

Unlike Yoni, though, this boy was bald. Yoni had never seen someone without hair before — even his baby sister who everybody said was bald had quite a bit of fluff topping her head. Yoni had heard of kids being bald, of course, and he knew that kids without hair were sick — really sick, with worse things than appendicitis. This knowledge didn't make the face-to-face meeting any easier. The boy was connected to more than just an IV pole. There were a couple of machines clicking and beeping quietly next to him.

The picture was altogether so frightening that Yoni stopped right in his tracks. His curiosity about the balloons forgotten, he opened up his mouth to say that he guessed he was in the wrong room and had better leave.

Before he could get a word out, the other boy spoke. "Hey! I didn't know there was anyone else on this floor! Anyone else *frum*, I mean."

Unsure of what to do, Yoni nodded.

"What's your name?" the other boy asked.

"Yoni. Yoni Feldman."

"I'm Eliyahu Kesser," said the boy in the bed. "Wanna sit down?"

Yoni sat. It was easier than finding an excuse to leave.

"How old are you?" the boy continued.

"Twelve. I'll be *bar mitzvah* in five months."

"Oh."

There was a short silence, which Yoni surprised himself by breaking. "How old are you?"

Eliyahu nodded toward the balloons in the doorway. "My *bar mitzvah* is tonight." His voice remained steady.

Yoni's jaw dropped. What a horrible thing, to be so sick and stuck in a hospital for your own *bar mitzvah*!

"Is anybody here with you?" he asked, then instantly regretted it. What if the answer was no?

He was relieved when Eliyahu nodded. "My father's here. He just left for Minchah. He's the only one here, because we live in a different city. My mother was supposed to come—she even had a plane ticket—but then all three of my little sisters got chicken pox and she had to stay home with them. So we'll be having a quiet celebration." His face was brave.

"Oh," Yoni said.

Eliyahu pointed to a pile of gaily-wrapped boxes in the corner, which had escaped Yoni's notice. "Those are all presents—from my friends and my aunts and uncles and grandparents. I'll unwrap them later. And my father's bringing supper from Kosher Delight—they're supposed to have really good food." He managed a grin. "Much better than the chicken at your typical *bar mitzvah*, anyway."

"Sounds nice," Yoni said. It really didn't, of course. It sounded terribly lonely and sad. But what else could he say?

The boy nodded and stared out the window. His mouth opened, and then closed again. He looked like he wanted to say something, but was scared.

Yoni wasn't sure if he should leave or not.

Eliyahu answered the question for him when he finally blurted out, "Do you want to stay for my party? I know it's not really much — and I know you're sick — but maybe, just for a little bit …."

Yoni hardly knew Eliyahu, and he wasn't at all sure what the party would be like, but one look at the other boy's face told him what his answer would be.

"Sure," he said. "It sounds great. My cousin's *bar mitzvah* is tonight and I couldn't go, so I'll come to yours instead." He decided that if Eliyahu could smile, he could, too.

Eliyahu's face lit up like a million-watt bulb. "We're gonna have fun," he announced joyously.

Yoni was sure that he was right, and neither boy was disappointed. Eliyahu called his father to inform him that there would be a guest at the party, while Yoni went to inform the nurse on duty as to his whereabouts, so as not to cause any alarm.

Before long, Eliyahu's father showed up bearing food from Kosher Delight, which filled the room with delicious smells. He greeted Yoni warmly, and Yoni suddenly felt right at home in the hospital room. This might not be your average *bar mitzvah seudah*, but Yoni knew it was going to be a memorable one.

Truth be told, with Yoni there, it really wasn't all

that different than any other *bar mitzvah*. There was a proud *bar mitzvah* boy, and there were friends and family — even if each was represented by only one person. Yoni may not have met Eliyahu until that night, but an hour into the party, he found himself singing with an enthusiasm he hadn't known he possessed. There was plenty of music. Eliyahu's father had brought along a lively *simchah* CD, and Eliyahu's friends had sent their own CD of *bar mitzvah* songs that they'd recorded themselves in their classroom.

Like Eliyahu had promised, the food was good, even though Eliyahu's father was the only one eating. Yoni was still on a mostly-liquid diet and Eliyahu didn't have much of an appetite, but the presence of the fancy meat and side dishes still made it feel like a real *bar mitzvah*.

When the eating and singing were over, Eliyahu offered to say a *p'shetel*. "Is it all ready?" his father asked, startled.

Eliyahu nodded, then turned to Yoni to explain. "I was working on it with my *bar mitzvah* teacher, and it was only half-done when I had to go to the hospital again. But I finished it up yesterday, by myself. It's probably not as good as it would have been, but …" He grinned. "It'll do, right?"

Eliyahu spoke clearly and confidently about mitzvos as the purpose of life, and the added significance his *bar mitzvah* had taken on in the face of his illness. The parts that he had written himself weren't too polished, but they were more meaningful than any speech Yoni had ever heard.

"That was awesome," he said earnestly when Eliyahu finished.

Eliyahu grinned. "It didn't hurt that I only had to tell it to two people. I was terrified to do it in front of a crowd. I guess I lucked out!"

Yoni smiled back. Only somebody like Eliyahu could find the good in a situation like this—lucking out, indeed.

Soon it was time to open the gifts. "This is a fun party," Yoni said. "Usually, you don't get to open presents at the party, but now you can!"

Eliyahu nodded with shining eyes as he unwrapped one package after the next. There were *sefarim*, books, shiny *Kiddush* cups, a fancy new watch and even a silver-plated *menorah*!

After carefully handing the last present—a beautifully bound edition of *Mishnah Berurah*—to his father to place on one of his shelves, Eliyahu turned to Yoni.

"You're the best one, though, you know that?"

"The best what?"

"The best *bar mitzvah* present. I thought I wasn't going to have any friends at my party, and then you came." His tone was matter-of-fact, but his face betrayed what Yoni's presence meant to him.

I'm important here, Yoni realized with a start. *I matter to Eliyahu, much more than I would have mattered to Moshe at his bar mitzvah, despite how close we are.*

The party wound down when two nurses entered the room. One checked on Eliyahu and gave him his medicines, while the other came to escort Yoni back to his room and run some tests on him.

"I'll stop in tomorrow before I leave," Yoni said as he started heading back to his room.

"You'd better," Eliyahu answered happily.

As Yoni slid carefully into his bed—he still felt sore and achy two days after surgery—the phone rang.

"Hello?"

"Hey, it's Moshe! The party's over, and I just wanted to let you know that I missed you tons!"

"I missed you, too," Yoni assured him, but he didn't have to work hard at sounding brave anymore.

"It must have been awful for you to be stuck in the hospital while the party was going on. Don't worry, though, I had Feivel save you a piece of the fanciest cake on the sweet table. It was really great. I wish you could have been there."

Yoni smiled and began to ask for details, but he knew that he wasn't truly sorry to have missed Moshe's *bar mitzvah.* If he'd been there, he would have missed the special *bar mitzvah* he'd experienced that night. Given the choice, he'd spend the night in the hospital all over again just to be at Eliyahu's *bar mitzvah*, where he truly mattered.

NEITHER HERE NOR THERE

"So what did you decide in the end, Zeesy? Are you coming with us to Brooklyn on Sunday?"

I looked at Riva and bit my lip. It wasn't that I didn't want to go with her, or that my mother needed my help on Sunday, or that I didn't like Brooklyn. It was just that my cousin Bashy had invited me to go along with her family to the zoo on Sunday.

And me? I couldn't make up my mind.

I hadn't given Bashy an answer yet, either. She'd told me several times the night before about how much fun we'd have, how the zoo had been recently renovated and was supposed to be stupendous, and how her parents were packing along a huge barbecue supper to eat in the park on the way home. But I still couldn't decide.

Now I was confronted by Riva, who was every bit as insistent as Bashy had been. "My aunt told me about this store that has the most amazing sales! And we're going to have a blast on the bus ride. Esther has the funniest book of riddles that she got from her older brother—we can read that the whole way!"

"I don't know …," I said. It sounded great. It really did. But so did spending the day in the zoo with my cousins.

"And we'll stop at this great dairy restaurant for lunch! It'll be so much fun!" Riva giggled.

I nodded. Riva sounded so confident. The only difference between us was that I had the opportunity to go to the zoo with family, and she didn't. And that difference was bothering me to no end.

"Why'd it have to be on the same weekend?" I complained to Rochel Leah on our way home from school. Rochel Leah is my best friend, and if she'd been coming along on the trip to Brooklyn, that *might* have helped me make up my mind. As it was, though, she had a family wedding on Sunday, so she didn't have to make any choices. I envied her for that.

Rochel Leah smiled. "I guess that's just the way things worked out. But don't worry—even if you have to miss out on something, maybe it'll be a comfort to you that I'm also missing out."

"But at least you don't have to *decide*!" I nearly wailed. "Your mother told you a month ago that you were all going to the *chasunah*, and that was that!"

I was annoyed when Rochel Leah laughed. "Oh, come on, Zeesy. What's the big deal already? Just pick one!"

I nodded. But … it *was* a big deal. Which one should I choose? My mind was whirling with the options as I pushed open the door to my house a few minutes later. I didn't stop pondering the momentous decision all through homework time, supper and the rest of the evening. I usually devoted my spare time at night to reading or talking on the phone. That night, though, I just paced in my bedroom.

Which should I choose? Quality time with family, seeing beautiful animals at the zoo, a simple but delicious barbecue in the park … or being with my friends, shopping like a grown-up, eating at some sophisticated restaurant … ?

I had a hard time falling asleep that night, and I woke up slightly bleary-eyed. But at last my mind was — tentatively — made up.

I was going shopping with my friends. I loved my cousins, the zoo and barbecues, but I'd gone to the zoo with my cousins before. I'd miss them and everything, but a day in Brooklyn with a few good friends would make me feel special.

As soon as I arrived in school, I set out in search of Riva.

"Hey, Riva!" I called across the classroom. "I decided to come with you on Sunday!"

I'd expected a happy comment and a huge smile, but I was disappointed. Riva's face kind of fell and she looked like she wasn't quite sure what to say. As I watched her, my smile faltered somewhat, too.

Riva finally found her tongue. "Zeesy, I ... uh, well, I just ... To tell you the truth, you didn't seem that interested yesterday, so I asked Hadassah to come along instead." The words came out in a rush. "My father's driving us in his van instead of us taking the bus, and we're just ... full. I wish you could come, but my father is *makpid* on everybody wearing a seat belt." She really did sound regretful.

It took a second, but I forced a smile to my face without too much difficulty. Hadn't I wanted this all along, to have the choice taken away from me and made by somebody else or by circumstances?

"That's fine," I told Riva. "It would have been great to go with you, but I was deciding between that and going on a trip with my cousins. I guess I'll be going with them to the zoo."

"Oh, good. I mean, I'm glad you have something fun to do instead. I hope it works out with your cousins."

"Oh, it will," I assured her confidently.

I waited until I got home from school to call Bashy.

"Hi, Bashy!" I said, as soon as I heard her voice on the

other end of the line. "Guess what? I'm coming with you on Sunday!"

For the second time that day, I was surprised by a long silence that just seemed to stretch and stretch.

"What's the matter?" I asked.

"Well, you said that your friends were going to Brooklyn. And ... well, I was pretty sure that you were going to decide to go with them. My father really wanted to bring in the van for a tune-up and oil change this weekend, and it sounded like you weren't coming, so he went ahead and took it in to the mechanic. We're going to take the car instead, and we'll be squashed in like sardines as it is, with the seven of us, so ..."

"Couldn't you get back the van in time?" My voice sounded heavy with disappointment, even to my own ears.

"I don't know ... Let me ask my father."

I clutched the phone tightly to my ear while I waited. By the time Bashy returned to the phone, the little lines on the edge of the receiver were etched into my palms.

As soon as Bashy got back on, I knew that the answer was no. "Sorry," she said, and she sounded every bit as sorry as Riva had earlier, "but my father said that the mechanic told him there was something wrong with the motor. He decided to fix it right then since the van was already in the shop, so half the engine is lying on the ground. It's not going to be ready until Monday, and the mechanic is off tomorrow. We can't even ask them to rush it, since there's nobody there to do the work. But, anyway," her voice brightened, "weren't your friends doing something on Sunday? Now you won't have to make a decision—you can go with them."

"I can't," I told her, not bothering to try and hide my frustration. "Somebody else decided to go with them and now there's no room for me." I sighed irritably. "Couldn't you have waited for me to let you know?"

"I'm really, really sorry," Bashy said sincerely. "It's just … you were taking so long to decide, and my father really wanted to take care of the car."

My irritation melted away. She was right. I had taken a long time to decide, and they had no obligation to take me along, anyway. It was nice of them to offer me the opportunity to come with them in the first place. I had nobody to blame—nobody except myself, that is.

I hung up the phone two minutes later feeling very sorry for myself.

I spent that Sunday morning moping around the house. All I could think of was the fun that other people were having. My cousins were almost certainly on their way to the zoo by now. The small car would be shaking with laughter and merriment as they drove along to the beat of a bouncy music tape. My uncle would be telling one side-splitting joke after another, while my aunt handed out bars of her famous homemade peanut oatmeal bars.

When I tore my mind away from my cousins, it wandered to my friends on their way to Brooklyn, giggling as they read riddles to each other and chatting about anything and everything of interest to a high school girl. Soon they'd be piling out of the van onto the busy streets, ready to enjoy their day.

And me? I picked up a book, stared at a page for a minute, and then put it back down. It was no use. I couldn't enjoy anything when I knew that other people were having so much fun without me. It wasn't jealousy exactly, but the bitter taste of what I *could* have been doing ….

It was my mother who interrupted my brooding.

"Zeesy, the boys really want to get out a bit, but the baby just got over a virus and I don't want to take him outside yet. Do you think you could take them somewhere for a little while—maybe to Pizza Plaza or Izzy's Ices?"

"The boys" were my three little brothers. Moishy was seven, Betzalel was five and Dovid was four. Now that my mother mentioned it, I realized that they *were* acting a little rambunctious. I'd been so wrapped up in my misfortune that I hadn't noticed what they were doing. Dovid was busy emptying out the little drawers in my mother's sewing desk, examining every item with deep interest, while Moishy and Betzalel were engaged in some wild form of hide-and-seek that involved racing madly around the house while whooping like wild Indians.

When my mother mentioned Pizza Plaza and Izzy's Ices, all activity ground to a halt. They gathered around my mother and me, talking loudly.

"I want pizza!" Moishy said.

"No! I want ice cream!" Betzalel argued.

"Yippee!" Dovid shouted.

"Quiet, please," my mother said softly. As usual, the boys were quiet. "Zeesy, do you mind taking them?"

"No," I said. I really didn't. I wanted to get out of the house so badly that it would be a relief to take my little brothers out. "Where should I take them?" I asked.

My mother smiled at me. "It's up to you, Zeesy. You're the one in charge, so you choose."

It was a major decision for me. It was a warm day outside and ice cream sounded really good. At the same time, I was hungry, and pizza would do a better job at sating my appetite. The boys were quick to take advantage of the weakness they saw in my hesitation.

"Ice cream!" Betzalel said.

"No! Pizza!" Moishy objected.

"Can't we have both?" Dovid asked.

I turned to my mother. "Could we have both, Ma?"

My mother paused for a second, then nodded. "Okay, as long as it's okay with you, Zeesy. I'll give you money for both. You can have one slice of pizza and one scoop of ice cream each."

Soon we were off. Our first stop was the pizza shop. Moishy had decided that we would go there first, and he'd convinced Betzalel that ice cream would taste better after pizza. I was glad that was settled so easily.

Then came the issue of ordering. The boys decided on their choices of pizza with dizzying speed.

"Plain," Moishy said.

"Plain," Betzalel said.

"Plain," Dovid said. I don't know if he knew the difference, or if he just wanted to be like his brothers.

All three boys and the man behind the counter looked expectantly at me.

And me? I couldn't decide!

My favorite was usually mushroom pizza, and they had half a pie of it right there in the glass display case, just waiting to be warmed up. It looked as mouthwatering as usual. Right next to it, though, were two lonely slices of the most delicious-looking broccoli pizza I'd ever seen.

Which would it be? Mushroom or broccoli? Broccoli or mushroom?

"Hurry up, Zeesy," Moishy whispered. "The man's waiting."

"I want my pizza already," Dovid chimed in.

"Whaddaya want, huh?" asked the man behind the counter, clearly impatient. A whole family with parents, grandparents and several kids in tow had just come in the door.

I couldn't decide, so I didn't—not really. I simply said, "Plain."

It was a non-decision; I was just following my brothers. Plain pizza was just fine, but it did nothing to improve my mood.

Neither did our trip to the ice cream store. I stood there looking into the huge tubs of ice cream. There was a dizzying number of choices. How would I ever decide on one?

My brothers, as usual, had no such problems.

"Mint chocolate chip," Moishy said immediately.

"Strawberry," said Betzalel, licking his lips.

"Chocolate," Dovid chirped.

Once again, everyone looked at me. I looked at the ice cream. Mocha swirl? Caramel? I just couldn't decide!

"Get the mint chocolate chip," Moishy urged me. "It's really good."

"Okay," I said. "Mint chocolate chip."

It was only when I was already holding my little cup of ice cream that I remembered I didn't really like mint ice cream. It tasted like toothpaste.

By the time we finished our ice cream, I was exhausted.

We set off for home. The boys looked happy and content, but I doubt I looked the same. I felt like I'd just run an obstacle course full of choices.

We were three blocks away from home when Moishy said, "Hey! Where's Dovid?"

I wheeled around. "He has to be here. Don't play tricks on me, Moishy!" But Moishy wasn't playing any tricks; Dovid was nowhere to be found.

I had no idea what to do. I mumbled out loud, "What should I do? What should I do?"

"Let's split up and go look for him," Moishy suggested.

"Run home and call the police!" Betzalel said.

"Quick!" they both said.

Suddenly, my mind cleared. Without even thinking, I told the boys, "Come quickly! We're going back to the store to see if we can find Dovid there. Maybe we left him behind by mistake."

"But maybe we'll find him faster if we look separately," Moishy said.

"No, we need to call the police! They'll look for Dovid," Betzalel insisted.

For once, I wasn't listening. "Come, boys! Quickly!"

They listened. We hurried over the pavement. I hadn't realized how far we'd come; now that I felt desperate, the walk seemed much longer.

"Let's check in these stores first," Moishy said as he pointed to a small strip mall. "Maybe he went in there to see if he could call home or something."

"No," I said, and I was so firm and decisive that I barely recognized my own voice. "We're going to check the ice cream store. That's the last place Dovid was seen — and the first place we'll check."

He was there. He was sitting at a table in the front of the store, licking a spoonful of black-cherry ice cream. "Dovid!" I exclaimed with relief.

The man behind the counter grinned. "Glad you're back. I was sure you would be before I had to try and track you down."

"Do I owe you money for the extra ice cream?" I asked.

"Nah," said the man. "That's on me."

"I want another one, too!" Moishy begged.

"And ...," Betzalel said.

To my surprise, I found myself speaking up. "Nope," I said. "We're going home." For once my mind was made up. My brothers listened right away and followed me out of the store without a peep of protest.

Suddenly, all the bad feelings that had accumulated over the day washed away. Something had changed. When Dovid was lost, I'd realized that there was an important decision to be made, and that it was up to me to make it. And I made the right choice. It made me feel hopeful that maybe it wasn't so hard to make decisions after all.

I was relieved to arrive home, until my mother announced that Tatty was taking us all out for dinner.

"Thanks for your hard work, Zissy," my mother said with a smile. "The restaurant is your choice. Burger Delight or Avi's Grill?"

For a second I felt panicky, but then I remembered that this wasn't hard after all. I smiled, thought it over and said, "Avi's Grill, please."

Then I headed to the kitchen for a nice cold drink. Nobody knew why I was grinning like I'd just won the lottery.

THE UNEXPECTED BIRTHDAY PRESENT

The summer that Benjy turned twelve was not an easy time for his family. Benjy's parents didn't discuss it with him — Benjy guessed that they didn't want to worry him — but the undercurrent of tension was there, hanging thick and heavy over the normally cheerful household.

Three months earlier, Benjy's baby sister had been born. Then, without any warning, Benjy's father had lost his job. Benjy's father had been called into his boss's office. The boss had sat him down, looking uncomfortable.

"Sam," he'd said. "I have something to tell you. I'm selling the company."

"Selling the company?" Benjy's father had repeated, uncomprehending.

"Yes. A firm down in Texas is going to buy it up and relocate down South. They offered to take any employees that I recommended. Any chance you'd want to follow the company to Texas with your wife and kids?" The boss had looked hopeful. He didn't want to be the bad guy who stranded his workers with no jobs and no pay. If they'd just be agreeable and move south along with the new firm, it would be a load off his own head and conscience.

Benjy's father had not wanted to take his family to Texas. "Texas?" he'd echoed to his wife over their dinner table that night. "As if a whole family can just pick up and move across the country. As if we have nothing tying us down here."

Texas was far away. Benjy understood that, even though he thought that it might be fun to move there. Benjy also understood that he had two sets of grandparents and countless aunts, uncles and cousins living within an hour's drive from their home. And he understood that while *Yiddishkeit* was blossoming in many out-of-town places, there were still huge advantages to living in his city that couldn't be found down South.

Some of these things Benjy understood by being told. Others he understood by listening to his parents' late-night conversations at the kitchen table, over steaming cups of tea or cocoa. And some he just understood on his own, because he was old enough to figure out many things by himself.

When the doors of his father's company closed for good a month later, Benjy was forced to understand even more things. His father had been looking for a new job for two weeks already, ever since his boss had informed him of the news. That day, his father sat him down and explained a few things to him. "There's no need to worry, Benjy," his father told him. "Hashem will take care of us, just like He always has until now. I'm going to do everything I can to find a new job, and we'll trust Hashem to make it happen at the right time. But in the meantime, we're going to have to be extra careful with our money. We're not going to be able to do everything we could in the past, and we'll all have to do our part to get through this."

Benjy told his father he understood, but he received his first blow when his parents told him that he couldn't go to camp that year. That's when it really hit home that things cost money. Well, of course he always knew that things cost money! But when money is tight, you start to understand that you are limited in what you can do.

Benjy couldn't sleep that night. He wasn't bothered so much by the news about camp itself, but the fact that his parents *couldn't afford* camp had opened frightening new possibilities in his mind.

There were so many things that cost money besides camp, like food. Benjy had overheard his mother talking about the inflated price of groceries even before his father lost his job! What if they had to eat peanut butter sandwiches every night for supper? Benjy thought about that, and decided he could live with it.

What about the other things that cost money? How would his parents pay rent? Would they have to move? What about buying new clothes and knapsacks and school supplies for the fall, which wasn't all that far off? And Benjy knew that babies cost a lot of money. Little Ahuva needed diapers and formula and medicine for when she got an ear infection. Well, at least Benjy was pretty sure that they wouldn't be getting rid of her ....

Benjy climbed quietly out of his bed and slipped into the large walk-in closet next to his parents' room, where Ahuva slept. He placed his finger in her tiny palm and watched as her tiny fingers curled around it. After a moment, he walked into the bedroom down the hall, where his other little sisters, Sari and Michal, slept soundly. It was comforting to watch them lying peacefully in their beds. It reminded Benjy that at least the most important things in his life would be together through thick and thin — like his family.

A few days later, Benjy remembered an upcoming event. He hadn't thought about it since the whole crisis started, since there had been so many other things to think and worry about. Next week was his birthday. He gazed at the ceiling of his room for a long time that night. No birthday had ever passed without Benjy receiving a present from his parents. He'd known what he wanted for months already. In fact, he'd even told his mother what he wanted. She'd responded to his request with a mysterious smile and a noncommittal "We'll see."

Benjy wanted a new watch, a fancy digital watch like some boys in his class were always showing off. It was an expensive watch, Benjy realized, as his eyes flickered over the eerie shapes that his furniture formed in the dark. Benjy understood without a shadow of a doubt that he couldn't expect his parents to buy him a present that year. But would his parents feel that they had to give him something?

It's not easy to give up on something you want. A twelve-year-old, only a year away from his *bar mitzvah*, is already nearly grown up. But even grown-ups often have trouble giving up on things ....

It was hard for Benjy to sit down at the table across from his mother the following night and say what he did. But he did it, because Benjy knew that he had to do his part.

"Ma?" he said, watching her sip her tea and flip through the circular of a local supermarket to see where she could find the best sales on groceries.

"Yes, Benjy?" she said, looking up with a smile. Benjy noticed the dark circles under her eyes — from worrying about money, and from getting up in the middle of the night to care for the baby.

"I just wanted to remind you that twelve-years-old is way too old for a birthday present." He'd considered not bringing up his birthday at all and hoping that his parents would forget about it since there was so much on their minds. He'd concluded that it was futile, though. Mothers always remembered birthdays.

His mother's smile faltered. "Is it really?" she asked quietly. "I seem to remember that you wanted a watch, Benjy. Maybe that will have to wait a little while this year, but ..." Benjy had been right. Mothers did remember birthdays.

"No, Ma, really. Birthday presents are for little kids. I didn't realize that when I told you about the watch. Besides, the one I got from Zeidy works fine."

"But Benjy, maybe—"

"And no party either, Ma, okay? Parties—and birthday suppers are really the same as parties—are for *really* little kids." Benjy figured that anything that tasted as good as hamburgers or pizza probably cost a lot more money than a regular supper.

When Benjy went to bed that night, he didn't feel happy—but at least he was at peace. He fell asleep almost as soon as his head hit the pillow.

—~—

Benjy woke up the morning of his birthday determined to pretend that it was a regular day, but he realized that he couldn't do that. It was his birthday, and nothing he did or didn't do could change that.

He came home from shul to find his mother in the kitchen, deftly flipping slices of French toast while the baby fussed in the infant seat in the corner.

"*Mmmm*," Benjy said, breathing in the rich smell of crisp bread and cinnamon.

"Happy birthday," his mother said. "I made it with lots of cinnamon and sugar, just for you."

Benjy grinned. "Thanks, Ma!"

The generous portion of French toast lifted his mood, which carried him happily out the door to see which of his friends were available to spend the day with him. He found that he could do nearly all the things in the city that he would have done in camp, had he gone away that summer. He usually learned in shul for an hour in the morning with Avi, and an hour at night with Moish. He went swimming with Naftali, whose family owned a pool. And he spent endless hours biking, hiking, and playing ball. It was turning out to be a pretty good summer after all — even without camp.

But because it was his birthday, the usual activities didn't seem quite so fun that day. While learning, Benjy had to fight to keep his attention focused on the page in front of him, and not let it wander off to the fun party his friends would have made him in camp. While playing with his friends, Benjy imagined a new watch glittering on his wrist as he deftly shot the ball up toward the basket.

"Want to get some ice cream now?" Naftali asked when

they tired of their game. "We can go swimming after."

Benjy shook his head. "Nah, I'll run home for lunch." Without much pocket money now, he usually went home when his friends decided to do anything that cost money. Any of them would have been happy to pay for him, but there was no way he would go along with them knowing that would happen. The fact that some of his friends had heard that his father had lost his job didn't make it any easier for him. The last thing Benjy wanted was pity.

Benjy would usually rejoin his friends in the afternoon. Today, though, Benjy said, "I'll see you tomorrow."

"What—no swimming?" Eliezer asked in surprise.

"I'm not in the mood today." It was true. Benjy was in the mood of doing something special, something different—something appropriate for his birthday. Swimming held absolutely no appeal.

Lunch—a plain old tuna sandwich—was eaten in pensive silence. There was nobody in the house. Benjy's father was out job-hunting and his mother was out shopping with the baby. Sari and Michal were at Benjy's aunt's house for the day.

When he finished his meal, Benjy left the house. He didn't know where he was going or what he was doing, but he didn't want to stay home. He grabbed his bike from the shed and set off slowly down the street.

He biked up one block and down the next, looking for something—anything—that would hold his attention and divert him from the images of parties and presents that were swirling through his head.

He found it unexpectedly.

Benjy was on a busy block in the shopping area of town. He rode slowly up the street, taking in the storefronts and watching people hurrying into and out of stores. He paused in front of a store that sold watches. Benjy knew it wasn't smart to dwell on something he wasn't going to get anyway, but he couldn't help himself. He gazed at one digital watch after another, watching their numbers flash against glowing faces.

There were several less expensive watches in the display window. Nearly identical to the fancier ones, they had slightly simpler faces and a few less features. Benjy knew that they'd probably last only a fraction as long, but … it was something. Maybe that … He tore himself away from the window and forced himself to move on. *No*, he told himself fiercely, *not even that*. A watch — any watch — was an extra. He wouldn't ask his parents for one. Birthday presents were silly, babyish, ridiculous. He used every adjective that he could think of to convince himself that he didn't want one.

He pedaled away just before his family's minivan pulled up in front of the store. He just missed seeing his mother hurry inside, her pocketbook on one arm and the baby on the other.

That was when it happened. Benjy was biking past

a flower shop when he glanced down at the ground. He braked in a whirl of dust. A flash of green and white was moving across the pavement, propelled by the breeze. Benjy dismounted his bike and grabbed it, then stared at his find in disbelieving silence.

It was a bill. A twenty-dollar bill. It was enough money to buy himself one of the watches he'd been staring at a couple of minutes earlier. It wouldn't be one of the more expensive ones, but it would still be a watch.

Did he have to return it? The thought ran quickly through his head, but Benjy had learned the *halachos* of *hashavas aveidah* that year. He remembered almost instantly that a single bill found on a busy street has no identifying *siman* whatsoever by which a previous owner could claim it. Benjy had every right to the twenty-dollar bill.

As if in a dream, he headed back to the store. He chained his bike to a pole and prepared to enter the store. His hand was on the door handle when he hesitated.

Was it right to use his windfall to buy something for himself? There were so many things his family could use, so many extras that they'd all been living without for the past month. How could he walk into the house with a watch that he'd bought just to give himself pleasure?

A little voice told him that he shouldn't spend the money on a watch. Another little voice argued angrily that it was his birthday. *You deserve it!* the voice yelled.

The hardest thing that Benjy had ever done was

unchain his bike and move away from the store for the second time that day. He rubbed the old leather watch that his grandfather had given him for his birthday three years earlier, and tried to remember the excitement he'd felt when he received it. It was a sturdy watch and as good as new. Why did he need another one?

Benjy biked around town for the rest of the afternoon, the twenty-dollar bill jammed tightly into his shirt pocket. He kept checking to make sure it was still there. By the end of the afternoon, Benjy's mind was made up.

He stopped by the grocery on the way home and selected a carton of vanilla fudge ice cream. It was something that his whole family would like. He would sneak the rest of the money into his mother's purse when she left it lying around the kitchen. She'd never know where it came from.

Once again, Benjy wasn't totally happy. How could he be when the images of the watches in the window still taunted him? *You could have had one of them*, whispered the voice in the back of his head. But somehow, despite the voice and the watches, Benjy was at peace.

Benjy wanted to make a quiet entrance into his house and spend time by himself before supper. He pushed open the door as quietly as he could.

"Surprise!"

Benjy dropped the ice cream and took an involuntary step back. He stared.

The living room was festooned with colorful decorations — much nicer than any of his friends could have dreamed up back in camp. There were no balloons or streamers, but bright chains made of construction paper that were clearly his sisters' handiwork, and a huge sign reading "Happy Birthday, Benjy" that took up half of the far wall.

"Look what we did!" shouted Michal, pointing at the decorations.

"Michal made the chains, and I made the sign," Sari told him. "I printed the letters and everything."

His parents stood behind the girls, beaming. "There's a special dinner waiting," his mother told him with a smile. "And there's something else for you by your seat."

Still disbelieving, Benjy moved slowly toward the table. There was a small gift-wrapped box at his place. He picked it up and opened it slowly.

It was a watch. A fancy digital one, with black numbers on a glowing face and a heavy black strap.

"But, Ma," he said, his voice coming out somewhat thick, "I told you I was too big for birthday presents."

His parents just smiled.

"I got something for everyone else, too," Benjy suddenly remembered. "Oh, no! I left it on the floor! It's gonna melt!"

Sari ran over to pick up the grocery bag. "Ice cream!" she shrieked. They hadn't eaten ice cream in quite some time.

Benjy's father looked at his son. "Where'd you get the money for the ice cream?"

Benjy told him.

"Twenty dollars," his father said slowly. "An unexpected birthday present. What did you use the rest for?"

Haltingly, Benjy pulled it out of his pocket and handed it to his father. "I was going to give it to you and Mommy — for groceries, or whatever."

Benjy's parents' eyes met over the table, which seemed incredibly festive even with plain white paper plates and napkins. Benjy's mother gave him a hug, and his father's voice, when he spoke, was as thick as Benjy's had been a moment earlier.

"The bottom line," he said, "is that some twelve-year-olds deserve a present — even if they're too old for them."

Benjy didn't know what to say, so he turned to Sari. "You'd better put that in the freezer so it doesn't melt," he said. He had a funny feeling that of all the birthday presents in the world, he'd really had the best one all along: his family. Love was something that you couldn't buy with money. Yes, he was sure of it; that was the best birthday gift in the world.

MEANS TO AN END

Elky's mother was talking on the phone and peeling carrots for soup when Elky came flying in the front door. She hurried to the kitchen and shifted impatiently from foot to foot while her mother tried to carry on her conversation. She was finding it hard to concentrate with her daughter hanging anxiously over her shoulder and flourishing a typewritten sheet of paper only inches from her face.

"Rina, I'd better go now. My kids are coming home from school, and I have somebody here who's making it very clear that she needs my attention." When she finally hung up, she turned to Elky with raised eyebrows.

"Elky, sweetheart, what in the world is so important? I haven't spoken to Tante Rina in ages …."

Elky didn't answer. She simply shoved the paper into her mother's hand, eagerness written all over her face.

Her mother read the paper slowly. "A poetry contest," she finally said thoughtfully. "Who's participating in this?"

"Every school in the city, Ma! This is major. And did you see what they're offering for first prize?"

Her mother frowned as she scanned the paper. "It says here that first prize will be a camera."

"Right! But it's not just any camera — it's a new digital one that does lots of really neat things. It's an amazing prize, Ma. And I plan on winning it." Elky spoke fervently.

"There are probably a lot of people who would like that prize — and a lot of people who are good at poetry," her mother commented. "Although you certainly have a way with words, Elky, keep in mind that there'll be plenty of competition. It's worth a try, but don't set your heart on it."

Elky just smiled. She knew there would be a lot of people working hard on the contest. But there was only one first prize, and she intended to be the one to win it.

It wasn't until after supper that Elky realized how much work was actually involved. She didn't have an idea for a poem yet, and there was no way she could start writing without one. She wandered from room to room, thinking hard.

"You have a whole week left till it's due," advised her older sister Miriam. "Why not forget about it for the night and wait for something to come to you?"

"Because I want it to be really, really good," Elky answered. "I can't wait until the last minute for an idea. I have to start on it tonight—not tomorrow!"

"Okay," Miriam shrugged, and returned to her book. Elky resumed her pacing. Why couldn't she just think of something already?

On her next round of the living room, Elky jumped as blaring music interrupted her musing. Her brother Meir was curled up on the couch near the boom-box.

"Meir!" Elky said. "Why is the music so loud? I can't hear myself think!"

Meir looked up from his book and pushed his glasses up his thin nose. "I like it loud," he responded simply.

"Well, do you mind making it a little quieter, please? I'm trying to come up with an idea and there's no way I can do that with music booming in my ears," Elky complained.

Meir sat up with a groan and reached over to turn down the volume. "You know, you could stay in your room if you want absolute quiet."

Elky scowled. "I didn't say I need absolute quiet—just a normal noise level. And last I was told, I wasn't in jail. I'm not exactly interested in staying cooped up in my bedroom all night because the rest of the house is too noisy."

Meir, bored of the whole conversation, allowed it to drop and directed his face right back into the book he had been reading. Within moments, all he was aware of were the plot he was immersed in and the music still playing happily — though more quietly than he would have liked — in his ear.

Elky, on the other hand, was a different story. When she tired of pacing, she sat down for a few minutes and buried her head in her arms. Why was it so hard to think of a meaningful, interesting subject for her poem?

"Elky," her mother called, "could you please run upstairs and read Sarale a bedtime story? The baby has food in his hair and desperately needs a bath, and I really can't spare the time right now."

"But, Ma," Elky exclaimed, "I'm still trying to think of an idea for my poem! I can't do that while I'm reading her a story!"

"Elky—"

"Wait, Ma. I bet Chevi will do it."

Happy-go-lucky Chevi was a year younger than Elky and not the best student. She was in the middle of studying for a history test and more than happy to take a break and read Sarale a bedtime story.

Meanwhile, Elky continued pacing, sitting and staring at the ceiling while she tried to come up with an idea. It came to her quite suddenly — a result of all that thinking. Why not focus on the *brachah* of *seichel* in her poem?

Without a mind to think and a mouth to speak, a person would be just like any other creature. She could compare a person to a treasure box, and write how a person is nearly useless without human intelligence, the treasure inside.

Her mind was spinning now, and Elky flew downstairs to work on her father's computer. When she got there, she discovered Leizer using it, playing what looked like a very boring game of minesweeper.

"I need the computer," Elky announced. She marched over to her younger brother and stood over him.

"Wha– Just a minute, hang on." Leizer's voice was tense. "I'm about to break my time record."

"I need it *now*."

"Just wait a second, okay?" Leizer's eyes were glued to the screen, his fingers flying over the mouse and keyboard. "I'm gonna break all the records on this computer—"

This is silly, Elky thought. *I'm going to lose my train of thought in a minute and my whole brainstorm will be for nothing. And this is just a silly old game of minesweeper, after all.* Elky reached out a hand and snatched the mouse.

"Wha– Elky!" Leizer yelled, lunging for her hand. "I need that. I'm about to break the time record!"

A short scuffle ensued. Leizer came out the winner, but the race for the time record was over. The clock on the computer had ticked its way into the next minute, and the moment was lost.

"I'm gonna—," Leizer said, looking furious.

"That game is such a waste of time," Elky said primly. "*I* need the computer for something important."

"But I was about to break my record!" Leizer bellowed.

Elky shrugged. "You shouldn't spend so much time on this game. You're on the computer every night. Is it so bad if I get to actually work on it once in a while?"

Leizer stormed out of the room, stamping his feet and making such a ruckus that Elky winced. But she immediately settled down to work, tapping away on the computer as she tried to get down her thoughts.

She was deeply engrossed in her work, trying to figure out how to best rhyme the endings of two lines, when she sensed someone standing behind her.

"Elky?"

It was her mother.

"Yes, Mommy?" Elky answered, turning to face her.

Her mother came around the desk, sat down on the chair across from Elky and just looked at her.

"Yes?" Elky asked. "Is something the matter?" She wasn't really focusing on her mother, though. She couldn't afford to lose her train of thought.

"I want to talk to you for a minute, Elky. Leizer just came to me in tears about a certain incident that he claims happened with the computer. Also, I still haven't managed to get Chevi back on track with her studying. And Meir's not looking too happy about the way his music was turned down." Elky's mother stopped speaking and simply watched Elky, who fidgeted as the last fragments of her thoughts faded into nothingness. It would take her at least ten minutes to recapture her ideas and get them down on paper. "Can you explain this to me, Elky?"

"Yes!" Elky exclaimed defensively. "I'm working so hard on this poem, and I need people to cooperate just a little if I want to succeed. Is that too much to ask?"

There was another long silence. Finally, Elky's mother continued, "I have a story to tell you."

There was nothing in the world that Elky wanted less at that moment than to hear a story, but she couldn't tell that to her mother. Elky frowned, crossed her arms and waited. The poem was practically forfeit for tonight, anyway.

"The contest that I was interested in had nothing to do with poetry," Elky's mother began. "I always considered creative writing to be just another school assignment. But I loved baking—boy, did I love baking!"

"You still do," Elky commented. She was beginning to be interested despite herself.

"*Mm-hmm.* And you'll probably still love writing in ten, twenty or thirty years. Anyway, here's what happened ..."

"Ma, could I have the kitchen tonight?" Chani asked eagerly, before she even had a chance to take off her coat.

"Hmm?" said her mother. "What do you need the kitchen for?"

"They just announced a cake decorating contest in school. The annual school tea for mothers is on Wednesday, and they didn't have enough volunteers to bake cakes — so they're asking eighth-grade students who like baking to help out! And they're making a contest out of it!" Chani's excitement was palpable. "So I figured that I'll bake the cake tonight and decorate it tomorrow — "

"Hang on a sec, Chani. I have a big bowl of challah dough sitting and rising right here on the counter. I really need to use the oven to bake that tonight. Why don't you bake tomorrow?"

"Oh … All right, I guess I don't really have much of a choice, then," Chani said disappointedly.

That night Chani looked through recipes. There was her mother's super mocha cake with rich chocolate glaze, but she was sure that there would be at least ten other chocolate cakes at the contest. It was too typical. How would a judge choose one over the others?

She could make pineapple upside-down cake, a family favorite — but it might be considered strange. Not everybody was used to putting pineapple in cakes.

Then there was her favorite carrot cake, with cream cheese frosting. But it seemed too old fashioned. Besides, she wasn't sure if the cakes were allowed to be milchig, and they didn't have any pareve cream cheese in the house.

As she continued to look through recipes, Zeldy walked

into the room. "Can I please have the index box? I need the recipe for chocolate chip cookies. We're having a siyum tomorrow, and Mommy said I could bake them in the toaster oven."

"Sorry, I'm using the box now." One of Chani's fingers was holding her place in the stack of recipes, and she didn't want to have to find it again. "Maybe in a few minutes — as soon as I finish looking for the perfect cake recipe for my contest."

"But I need it now. Mommy said I have to make them right away, so I can be in bed in an hour."

"So find a different recipe for chocolate chip cookies," Chani said impatiently. "There's one in every cookbook!"

Zeldy frowned, but nodded and headed off to find a cookbook with a good recipe for chocolate chip cookies.

Chani flipped to another index card in her mother's recipe file and paused. Strawberry shortcake! That was it! Everyone loved strawberry shortcake. It wasn't boring or old fashioned, and it would be different than the other cakes. She pictured a crowd of admiring faces gathered around her cake, which was piled high with fluffy white icing and a cluster of bright red strawberries in the center.

Chani puttered around the kitchen for a few minutes, making sure that all the ingredients she needed were on hand. Then she left to do some homework. She came back to the kitchen a while later to make sure that the strawberries she'd seen in the freezer would be enough for her cake.

Chani was just in time to see Zeldy remove the pan of

cookies from the toaster oven and hear her anguished cry. "Oh, no! They came out all flat and burned. All the cookies ran together—it's just a big mush in the pan!"

Their mother, who was clearing out the dishwasher at the far counter, stuck a mug in the cabinet and came over to look. "Did you use the recipe we always use?"

"What, the one in the file box? No, I couldn't use that one, because Chani was using the file box for something important." Zeldy spoke sarcastically. "I took a recipe from the big red cookbook on the middle shelf."

"Oh. I never use that cookbook for cake or cookie recipes unless I know somebody who's already tried it. It's very unreliable."

"I didn't know that," Zeldy said. She sounded near tears as she looked down at the pan of burnt cookies.

"Chani, you should have at least checked what cookbook she was using. You knew that the red one doesn't have the greatest cookie recipes. And honestly, I don't see why you couldn't have taken a minute to give her the card she needed."

"Sorry," Chani muttered. Honestly, what did everyone expect? She had a contest coming up! These were just cookies for some silly little siyum. Chani filed the recipe for strawberry shortcake in the front of the cake section of the file box, so she could take it out easily the next night. Then she headed up to her bedroom, satisfied with her progress.

The next night, supper was served late. Chani had started mixing the cake batter as soon as she came home.

It took longer than she thought it would, and soon her brothers and sisters were marching into the kitchen and asking for supper.

"As soon as Chani's done with the oven," her mother kept saying. By the time supper rolled around, everyone was in a less-than-great mood—and they blamed the late meal on Chani.

"Why didn't you just wait till after supper to bake?" Shimmy asked unhappily.

"Yeah, I'm starving," Zeldy added.

"I have a meeting tonight," Chani's father said. "At seven-thirty. I need to eat by seven so that I can get there on time," he added, with a sharp glance at Chani.

In the end, it was a hungry, rushed supper for everybody. But, Chani thought, at least she had the two layers of cake all baked and ready to be frosted, stacked and decorated.

The decorating would take some time, though ….

"Ma," she said, "I need to put together the whole cake tomorrow night. It's going to take me a long time. Maybe we could have pizza for supper?"

"All right," her mother answered, though she didn't look too happy. "I guess that's a lot better than what happened tonight."

The end of the next evening found the cake beautifully decorated, just the way Chani had envisioned, with tufts of white cream all around the cake and a bouquet of berries in the center.

"Chani, can I please come into the kitchen now?" Shimmy asked irritably.

Chani had banned her siblings from entering the kitchen after Shimmy and Yaakov had come in engaged in a cheerful wrestling match. She feared for her cake's safety. Now she said in her best drill sergeant voice, "All right. But no running. And watch out for the cake, or you'll be in huge trouble!"

―――

Elky's mother paused, and Elky looked up.

"So how did the story end? Did you win the contest?"

"I probably would have … if the cake had made it there."

"What?!"

"As I was on my way to the car the next morning, carrying the precious cake, somehow — I'm still not sure if I tripped on anything other than my own two feet — I ended up on the ground. The first thing I saw when I sat up was my cake lying two feet away. It was a total mess. The cover of the cake box had come off and the side of the car was splattered with whipped cream."

"You must have felt horrible!"

"I did. And the worst part of the whole thing was realizing how upset I'd made everyone in my family while I was focused on winning the contest. I'd really inconvenienced people, made them feel upset and hungry and nervous—and what did I have to show for it? Not even a cake! It made me realize how important it is to pay attention to how we do things, and not just the end result. I had a teacher back in high school who used to drill that into us—that the end does not always justify the means!

"If I'd done the cake project the right way—making sure not to bother or inconvenience other people—then all I would have lost was the cake. As it was, I felt like I'd lost the contest, the cake, three full nights and a lot of good feelings. It was the last loss that was the hardest to swallow."

There was another silence, and then Elky's mother stood up. "Well, that story was sitting in the back of my mind, waiting to come out, so I thought I'd share it."

Elky nodded slowly.

The next night found Elky working hard on her poem. She was interrupted several times by requests to have a turn on the computer, to read a story, to pour a drink. Each request was met with a smile and cheerful service.

Meanwhile, a new file had been opened on the computer. Elky had decided to switch topics for her poem.

Now she was writing about getting things done—and how the end doesn't necessarily justify the means.

There was no way to know if she'd win the contest. But Elky wanted to make sure that she wouldn't lose anything else—anything more important—along the way.

A FRESH START

It was a long, freshly painted hallway, and it reminded Dudy of the school hallway back home — that is, where his family used to live. He had to tell himself fiercely that he *was* home, in this new city and in this new school.

Not that school last year had felt very homey to him either …

The classroom at the end of the hall — that was where he had to go. Dudy's hands were suddenly sweaty, and his mind swam with memories that he'd tried hard to repress all summer. It was early, twenty minutes before the buses were due to arrive, and there was hardly anyone in the halls. Dudy had asked his father to drive him to school, just this once. It would delay his meeting with his new classmates — not indefinitely, but at least for an extra half hour.

Maybe somebody was already in the classroom, though. Without thinking twice, Dudy turned the handle of a door right next to him, marked "Supplies Closet." The door swung open, and Dudy disappeared into the tiny, black room with its jumble of tools and cleaning supplies.

He cautiously felt his way over to a wall and sat down. The memories from last year, from his old school, came fast and furious now. He remembered all the mischief he had made. He remembered his *rebbi* looking at him from across his desk, genuinely upset at him for his misbehavior, and the way he had brazenly stared back at his *rebbi*, showing no outward signs of the fear he felt inside. The faces of his classmates, first shocked and then filled with a terrible curiosity as, eyes gleaming, they watched to see what their *rebbi* was going to do to Dudy this time.

His mind fast-forwarded to the scene that followed, in the principal's office. The hard floor of the supplies closet reminded Dudy of the feel of the orange plastic chair across from the principal's desk. The principal was pacing back and forth, talking, but Dudy wasn't really listening; he couldn't even remember what Rabbi Weiss had said to him. He remembered the principal sitting down across from him and looking him full in the face; he remembered the mixture of understanding and compassion and sternness in his eyes. Dudy remembered how he'd looked away from the principal, unwilling to listen or accept.

He remembered coming home afterwards to a quiet, empty house, nobody home with whom he could share his frustration and pain—but there Dudy's mind balked. Those memories were too painful. He didn't want to go there, couldn't afford to go there, not on his first day in a new school.

"Hey, who's there?" The voice was cautious and soft, and it came from the other side of the closet. Dudy tensed, his hands clenching into fists as he peered into the darkness and tried to make out a face or form. He couldn't. The little light filtering in under the door only allowed him to see the dark outlines of several tools stacked nearby.

There was something familiar about that voice, though. Dudy remained quiet, ready to run. He felt angry. Couldn't anything ever work out right for him? He couldn't even find some privacy in a closet!

"Don't be dumb," said the voice. "I saw you come in. I know you're there." In a flash, Dudy knew why the voice sounded familiar—but he couldn't be right. It had to be a figment of his overactive imagination, a product of fear and nervousness. Well, in a moment he'd find out for sure.

"My name is Dudy Myerson," Dudy answered. His voice, to his own ears, sounded cold and detached.

"Dudy!" Dudy's heart fell as he realized he was right.

He couldn't imagine why Avigdor Cohen was hiding in a supplies closet in some school in New York, but it was definitely Avigdor's voice. "It's Avigdor. Avigdor Cohen."

"I know," Dudy answered in the same cool voice.

"You knew I was in here?" Avigdor sounded surprised, and Dudy could hear something else in his voice. A sort of catch. Had Avigdor been *crying*?

"No, but when you talked, I knew it was you."

"Oh," Avigdor answered.

There was a long silence. Dudy seethed silently over the unfairness of it all. Everyone had spoken to him about making a fresh start, a new beginning, forging a new path of trying hard and succeeding. How in the world could he make a new start with Avigdor here?

"What are you doing in New York?" Dudy finally asked.

"My father moved here this summer. After he got remarried."

Against his will, Dudy was suddenly filled with a surge of pity for his old classmate. He'd been so close to a life like that himself last year—a life without a mother. Now his mother was back at home, nearly back to herself, and things were almost normal again. And yet, the turbulent waves of last year were still chasing him. He couldn't imagine how Avigdor felt after living with his grandmother for two years, never being quite the same as everybody else … and now being uprooted and planted in New York. He must also be hoping for a new start.

This time it was Avigdor who broke the silence. "Wanna make a deal?" he asked.

"A deal?" Dudy echoed curiously.

"Yeah. Don't say anything about me to anybody in the class, and I won't say anything about you."

Dudy couldn't see Avigdor's face in the dark, but he pictured him in his mind: on the short side, with dark glasses and intense brown eyes. Yes, Avigdor would keep his word. Dudy was filled with a sense of relief.

"Deal."

They emerged together from the closet a few seconds later — Dudy with his shoulders thrown back, staring at the world with defiant eyes, and Avigdor with his head down.

"Hey, don't look so depressed, all right?" Dudy said. The way Avigdor looked — nervous and beaten — reminded him of the way he felt inside, even if he didn't show it.

Avigdor looked up with the shadow of a smile on his face. Their eyes met, and it suddenly dawned on Dudy how similar they were. Their differences lay in how they dealt with adversity, and those differences had kept them miles apart last year. Dudy had made more trouble and spoken with more *chutzpah* than any other boy in their class. He'd spent his recesses playing hard and acting tough. Avigdor, on the other hand, had kept mostly to himself. He'd been a genuinely good kid; he tried to avoid Dudy so he wouldn't get involved in his plots, but he didn't particularly rejoice in his downfalls either.

They were an interesting pair to have just struck a serious deal, but that was the way things had worked out. They arrived together at the door of their classroom.

"Ready?" Dudy asked with feigned nonchalance. He was sure Avigdor could see right through it.

Avigdor swallowed hard and nodded. Dudy pushed open the door.

~

Being good, Dudy discovered, was almost as easy as being bad — especially when things were pretty normal at home. Now that his mother was around to help him and the dining room table was shiny and free of clutter, it wasn't all that hard to do homework. And when his homework was done and he was well prepared for class, it wasn't that hard to pay attention and answer questions.

During the first several days of school, Dudy kept an eye out for Avigdor. Somehow, their meeting in the supplies closet and the deal they had struck made them into allies. Dudy found himself walking Avigdor halfway home after school and making sure that he was having a nice time during recess.

The two boys didn't seem likely to become better friends, though. They were too different. Dudy still enjoyed spending recesses playing hard and working off all the physical energy that built up during class. Avigdor never seemed to have very much energy to work off. There were a couple of quieter boys in the class who usually hung out in the classroom during recess, talking and sometimes trading stamps or reviewing their notes. After a couple of days, Avigdor was comfortably absorbed in their group, and he looked perfectly content.

Both boys were happy. They'd left behind a stormy year and entered into a period of calm, and they were trying to make the best of it. Nobody knew about the past storm—nobody. At least, not in the beginning of the school year.

Dudy was completely unprepared when it happened one rainy morning. The previous day had been so beautiful and sunny that Dudy had barely managed to get home and eat supper before he found himself outside again, biking to the nearest city park with a couple of new friends. After dark, he'd called home to ask for permission to go with his friends to a nearby ice cream store. Dudy's mother had asked about homework, and Dudy had groaned.

"Come on, Ma, please," he'd begged. "I'll get to work on it as soon as I come home."

By the time he came home, though, his father was

leaving for Maariv, and the learning session they shared afterwards did nothing to prepare him for the verbal *halachah* quiz his class was having the next day.

Dudy had planned to wake up early and study, but when he woke up the room was way too bright. He must have shut off his alarm clock in his sleep. It was all Dudy could do to get to school on time; there was no time to study.

Dudy did terribly on the verbal quiz. The *rebbi* called on him three times, and each time Dudy stammered through an incorrect answer.

By his third try, the *rebbi* lowered the sheet of questions and looked at Dudy disapprovingly.

Dudy colored and looked down. He looked up a moment later, startled, at the whisper coming from behind him.

"C'mon, Myerson, aren't you going to do something?" Shua, the guy who sat behind Dudy, hissed.

"Huh?" Dudy whispered back, confused.

"Y'know, like the trouble you used to make in your old school? Talking back to the *rebbi*, storming out of the classroom … We heard all about it — don't think we don't know. Aren't you going to do the same thing here?" Shua's eyes were lit up with the same kind of indecent anticipation that Dudy had often glimpsed in the eyes of his former classmates.

Before Dudy could even begin to recover from Shua's

comment, there was another whisper from across the aisle.

"Hey, what's going on, Dudy? Softening up?"

Dudy blinked in bewilderment as he looked at Binyamin—and found the *rebbi* talking to him once again.

"Dudy, please. Enough disturbance. If you don't know the answers, at least sit quietly in your seat. If you can't do that, I'll have to ask you to leave."

But Dudy hadn't done anything! His anger rising, Dudy suddenly felt a desire to make a scene, throw one of his notebooks on the floor, run out of the room and slam the door so hard that the windows would rattle in their panes. With an effort, he controlled it. *That was last year—last year's behavior, last year's feelings.* But had this year suddenly turned into a remake of last year?

His feelings were still the same. And his classmates' half-disdainful and half-respectful attitudes regarding his potential misbehavior were also the same.

Only one person could have given away his secret.

Only one person had followed Dudy to this new yeshivah and knew every last sordid detail of his past performance in school.

Only one person could have ruined everything.

The anger that had risen inside Dudy was suddenly directed at Avigdor. How could he have done such a thing? How could he have ruined a year that was off to such a promising start, the kind of year that Dudy had been dreaming of the whole summer? After all, they'd made a deal on the first day of school.

Avigdor was sitting close enough to Dudy to overhear his exchange with the other boys. If Dudy had turned around, he would have seen the shocked and compassionate expression on Avigdor's face. Avigdor couldn't have looked more upset if it had been his own secret history that had been revealed. But Dudy didn't look in Avigdor's direction, and he didn't see.

More than anything else, Dudy wanted to tell the class all about Avigdor. *Let him find out how it feels to have your side of the deal broken, to have everyone in the class know things about you that you least want them to know ....*

But a deal was a deal, and even though Avigdor had broken his side of it, Dudy just couldn't bring himself to do the same. When it was time for recess, the last thing Dudy wanted to do was play outside with his classmates. No, that wasn't the last thing. It would be worse to stay in the classroom and watch Avigdor and his goody-goody friends put their heads together and discuss him in hushed whispers.

Once again, Dudy sought refuge in the supplies closet. This time, he was very much alone in there. He spent the whole recess wrapped in a cocoon of misery. When the bell rang, he considered staying inside the closet until the class was well underway, then slipping out of the building and heading home ... but he resisted the urge. Everyone expected him to do that. He wouldn't give them the satisfaction of meeting their expectations.

He peeked through a crack to make sure nobody was around to see where he'd spent his recess, and then he quietly slipped out. Let them wonder ....

Avigdor spent the rest of their morning classes trying to get Dudy's attention. When he whispered Dudy's name, Dudy kept looking steadily at their *rebbi*, even though his mind was anywhere but on the lesson. Avigdor passed notes to Dudy, but they were left lying in the corner of Dudy's desk, unopened. When lunchtime rolled around, Dudy grabbed his lunch bag from his knapsack, swept up the small pile of notes and dumped them straight into the garbage can in the corner of the classroom.

He then headed out of the classroom and looked for a place where he could eat lunch undisturbed. He found the perfect spot in an empty classroom; the eighth grade was out on a field trip that afternoon. He sat in the corner, out of sight of the door. Nobody would ever think to look for him there.

It was a lonely day for Dudy. Every minute of his free time was spent hiding. He was hiding from the class; from Avigdor, the lowly traitor; and from the image of himself that he was trying so hard to escape.

Class was torture. Every time Dudy heard a whisper, he was sure it was about him. Every time a classmate turned to a friend and smiled, Dudy was sure that he was the butt of a private joke.

Dudy couldn't have been more relieved when the day was over. He snatched up his knapsack and was out of the classroom in seconds. He didn't look behind him, or he would have seen Avigdor racing down the hall after him, face set and shorter legs pumping to keep up.

Dudy set off toward his house at a rapid clip. He thought about what to tell his parents. Could he switch schools? It had been hard enough getting him into this one, he knew, with last year's history. But how could he stay there, knowing what the other boys thought of him?

His thoughts kept turning to Avigdor. He'd thought that Avigdor was a friend of sorts. He'd been looking out for *him*. Instead, Avigdor had betrayed him!

While these angry thoughts raced through his head, Dudy rounded a corner and came face to face with the very subject of his thoughts. Avigdor stood in the middle of the sidewalk. He suddenly didn't look little and timid. His face was determined as he faced Dudy.

Without a word, Dudy made an about-face and set off in the opposite direction.

"Just one second." Avigdor's voice was sharp. "Just listen to me, Dudy, all right? Just listen."

Dudy hesitated and stopped. He turned to face Avigdor.

"It wasn't me. I don't want to tell you exactly how they found out because it's *lashon hara*, but someone in the other class is related to a guy in our class back home, and he told him all about you. And about me, too, if that makes you feel any better."

"Why should I believe you?" Dudy couldn't believe how raw and pain-filled his voice sounded.

"Because we made a deal. Because you know me. That's all."

Was that enough? Dudy hesitated.

"All right." Dudy was surprised to find himself speaking. He didn't even realize that he'd already made up his mind.

"Good," said Avigdor. "Because I could have thought the same thing about you, you know, when the guys started talking about me. But I didn't. Because we're both trying to make a fresh start. Because we made a deal, and because ... well, it *is* right before Rosh Hashanah."

"Yeah," Dudy said slowly. It really was the season for fresh beginnings. He'd known that he needed a fresh start in behavior and schoolwork. He hadn't realized that he'd have to learn how to trust others, too. "Well, I guess I'm ready to start, if you are."

Avigdor grinned. "I sure am. Dudy?"

"Yeah?"

"My … uh, my stepmother just baked honey cakes today, and she told me this morning that she was going to need a taste test done tonight. Wanna come over for a few minutes?"

Dudy hesitated, and then nodded. "Sounds good." Fresh starts could include friendships, too — no matter how unlikely. As the two boys headed down the street together, it seemed to both of them that the future was hovering before them, ready for them to leap into it with everything they had.

LOOKING IN THE MIRROR

It was the precise timing of the events of that Wednesday, Henny thought later, that turned the day into a wild roller coaster. The events themselves weren't so turbulent, but the feelings they caused were.

The day had started out—as most days do—pretty neutrally. Henny woke up, got ready for school, helped her little sister Bassy locate her lost shoes, ate breakfast and left for school right on time.

Henny usually walked to school alone. Today, though, when she rounded the corner of her block, she found somebody waiting. It was Chayala Shapiro, and the big, friendly smile on her face made it very clear that she'd been waiting for Henny.

"Hi, Henny!" Chayala said cheerfully. "How are you?"

"Fine, *baruch Hashem*," Henny answered politely. "What's up?" It was obvious that something was, since Chayala lived almost four blocks away and they never walked to school together.

"The story you wrote for the school newspaper last month—that's what's up!" Chayala answered, falling into step with Henny. "Henny, I can't even tell you how grateful I am."

"Uh, why?" Henny asked. Her mind began spinning frantically, trying to remember what she'd written about last month. She wrote a short story for the school paper every month, and last month's paper was already old news to Henny. There was another issue coming out that morning, which would be delivered to all the classes in their school just before morning recess. And Henny was already busy with the story for *next* month's paper, which was due in just two weeks. How could she be expected to remember a story from last month?

"You know how Mina had that huge argument with her neighbor?"

Aha! Henny thought. Chayala was talking about the Mina story. "Uh-huh," she answered, with mounting curiosity. "What about it?"

"You will not believe this," Chayala said, "but I had exactly the same type of argument with my friend yesterday. About almost the same thing! And I was about to do the same thing that Mina did, when I remembered your story."

By now, Chayala had completely captured Henny's interest. She looked expectantly at Chayala.

"So I didn't," Chayala continued. "I remembered what Mina learned and I held myself back. And you know what? The whole argument died down really quickly, and I was so happy later — and I felt so good about myself. But really, it was all because of you and your story, Henny!"

"Really? Thanks! That's so good to hear!" Henny answered. She felt her cheeks flush warm with pleasure, and a little embarrassment, too. She'd just started writing for the paper at the beginning of the year and wasn't completely used to the compliments and publicity yet. But it really *was* good to hear. In fact, the feedback from Chayala gave her a warm, fuzzy feeling that lasted her throughout the cold walk to school.

The happy feeling followed her into the classroom and throughout the first two classes of the day, until it was time for recess. And then the two editors of the school newspaper walked into the room, proudly bearing tall stacks of crisp, neatly stapled papers. They counted out the correct number of newspapers, as girls crowded around them eagerly. The taller of the two, Dafna, caught Henny's eye over the group of girls reaching for their copies.

"Nice work this month, Henny," she said. "Really nice."

There was an increased surge of interest. After all, there was something special about having a classmate write a steady column for the school newspaper, especially when you were only in ninth grade.

Henny didn't like standing there in the room and watching other people read her story right in front of her eyes. She wasn't sure why. Was she was afraid of seeing a hint of dislike or disapproval in someone's expression as they looked at her work? Or was she just embarrassed at all the attention?

Either way, the classroom was not her favorite place to be just then, so she signaled to her best friend, Efrat, and the two of them left the classroom together.

"I hope everyone likes my story," Henny commented. "I'm always scared that people will think it's really dumb or something, and everyone will just keep on telling me that they like it because they don't want me to feel bad."

"Nah, I doubt that will happen," Efrat answered. "You showed me your story, and it was really good."

"But what if it does happen? How will I know?" Henny wondered out loud. "People wouldn't tell me, would they—just like you'd never tell someone that she did a bad job at something or that she's wearing a really ugly outfit."

Efrat shrugged. "I don't think you have to worry about that." Henny noted that she looked a little preoccupied, as if she was worried about something, but her observation was quickly replaced by the same excited, nervous thoughts about her story.

"Do you think my characters are developed enough? Is there a plot? Tell me the truth, Efrat! I'm so scared that people aren't going to like this one."

"I'm telling you," Efrat said. If there was some tiredness and a certain disappointment in her voice, her best friend didn't notice. "It's *not* going to happen."

And it didn't. In fact, as soon as Henny walked into the classroom after recess, she was besieged by compliments.

"Henny, I don't know what it was about that story, but it just *worked*, you know what I mean?"

"Henny, did you base that story on me or something? I felt like it was totally talking about me!"

"I'm bringing this one home to show my mother. She'll love it!"

Henny's face grew hot and she smiled back at everyone, a little uncomfortably. She mumbled a few "thank yous" before slipping into her seat next to Efrat. Inwardly, though, she was glowing. She really *had* done it. Her writing was impacting people, making a difference. Henny thought about her English teacher, who had encouraged her to send something in to the school paper. She'd told her that there were good things she could do with her writing, and now Henny felt like she was finally doing them.

It was a great feeling, the feeling that comes from

having a talent and using it not only for one's own enjoyment, but to serve others as well. That great feeling lasted all day—or, rather, until five minutes after the final bell of the day.

Henny and Efrat walked side-by-side as they left the school parking lot and headed toward home. They didn't usually walk to school together, because Efrat lived just three blocks away from school and liked to walk slowly, yet always got to her classroom in time for the first bell, while Henny lived five blocks away from school and usually came flying into the classroom just ahead of the teacher. In the afternoons, though, neither girl was in a big rush to get home, and they matched their steps companionably, until they'd reach Efrat's house and Henny would continue on alone.

Today, though, the two girls could have been in different worlds as they walked. Efrat was frowning slightly, her brow furrowed and her head bent over in concentration, or maybe unhappiness. She was quiet.

Henny, on the other hand, was only walking sedately because she was already in ninth grade and didn't feel that skipping in a public street was proper. She couldn't stop thinking of the wonderful hit that her story had made, the rave reviews that she'd collected, and the warm feeling that she was really and truly making a difference. She just had one last question—a relatively minor one, really—about the plot.

"Efrat," she said, "what do you think about the way I ended it? Was it too —"

She never finished her sentence.

Efrat whirled on her, face pinched and eyes flashing with anger. "Was it too *what*?" she snapped, as Henny drew back and stared at her with wide, surprised eyes. "Honestly, can't you think about anything else? Haven't you even noticed that maybe there's something bothering *me* for once — or is it not that *important*, if it's not part of one of your wonderful stories?" Her voice was uncharacteristically sarcastic.

"But … but you didn't tell me!" Henny exclaimed. "How was I supposed to know?"

"*How* were you supposed to know?" Efrat mimicked. "Maybe by using your eyes, or your ears, or something! I can't believe that you actually wrote a story about that a couple of months ago! Remember that character — I think you named her Mina — who never gave a hoot about what her friends were thinking, because she never even cared enough to notice?"

"But I do care!" Henny protested earnestly. "I was just preoccupied, I guess."

Efrat snorted. "That's exactly the point. You're too preoccupied to notice anything important. And I really thought that was the idea of the story. Do you read what you write, or do you only write the stories for other people?"

Henny opened her mouth to answer, then shut it. Efrat's words stung. And what, really, was the answer? Did she really have only a mind for herself and her own petty concerns? Did she, as Efrat had said, not give a hoot about what her friend was thinking?

The rest of the walk to Efrat's house passed in uncomfortable silence. They were at Efrat's walk before Henny dared to ask, "Efrat? So what *is* bothering you?"

"Now you ask," Efrat answered bitterly. "Well, never mind now. Maybe some other time. Good night." Henny watched her best friend stalk across the grass.

The thoughts that besieged Henny on the solitary part of her walk home were no longer nervous and excited. Was she really so self-centered? Efrat was right; that *had* been the focus of her story two months ago. She'd wanted to show how people can be so involved in the minor ups and downs of their own lives that they can forgot to pay attention to their friends' feelings, too. And now Efrat had caught her doing exactly that.

It was painful, to realize that you've been doing something you've basically instructed others not to do. And it was embarrassing, as if she'd been caught doing something terrible …. Or maybe she really *had* been caught doing something terrible. It made Henny blush inwardly. She felt as if a part of her would like to just run away and hide.

Henny was still feeling uneasy when she arrived home. She left her knapsack sitting on the floor just outside the hall closet. She'd been carrying the new edition of the paper home separately, in her hands. Now, though, she didn't want to look at it for a while. She placed it down on top of her knapsack with a bit more force than necessary.

"Hi, Ma!" she said, putting on a cheerful face and poking her head into the kitchen. "Hi, guys!" she addressed her three younger brothers, who were sitting around the kitchen table and eating cookies with milk. It was a sure sign that supper wouldn't be ready for a while.

"How was your day, Henny?" her mother asked.

"Okay," Henny answered noncommittally.

"Why don't you take a couple of cookies? We'll be eating late tonight."

"Uh … no, thanks, not right now. Maybe in a few minutes." It was funny. Henny remembered feeling hungry when she left school, but her appetite had disappeared. She figured that the best thing she could do was distract herself with some homework. Then she could think about her problem later; it might be clearer to her then.

But something else happened before "later" came along. When Henny came downstairs for supper, she passed her brother Gedalya, only two years younger than her, sitting cross-legged on the floor and bent over her school paper. No wonder. She'd left it in plain sight and Gedalya was a bookworm if ever there was one. Well, at least somebody seemed to be enjoying the story …

As Henny walked by, Gedalya looked up suddenly. "Did you really write this?" he asked, pointing down at her name on the page.

Henny glanced down, then nodded. "That's right."

"Nice," he said with a laugh that somehow made Henny feel very uneasy. "Real nice. I can't believe *you* wrote *this*!"

"Why?" she asked.

"Because it's about not getting angry! As if you're the one to talk. Do you remember last week, when somebody walked into your bedroom without knocking while you were on a *very* personal and private phone call?"

Henny blushed scarlet. She certainly did remember. That had definitely not been one of her better moments.

"And you're actually writing about anger!" Gedalya rocked back and forth on the floor, cackling merrily.

This time, Henny controlled herself. She walked calmly out of the living room, all thoughts of supper forgotten, and headed back to her bedroom. There, she laid down on her bed and thought for a good five minutes, until she reached a decision. But the implementation of that decision would have to wait until after supper.

Henny felt as if her supper was the last meal of a condemned girl. She'd been so happy with her writing, with her status as writer for the school paper—maybe a little too happy. Soon that would just be a memory.

After supper, Henny pulled out a phone book and

looked up a number. "Hi, can I please speak to Dafna?" she said when somebody picked up. Her voice sounded a bit squeaky to her ears. She wasn't used to calling twelfth graders.

"Hello?" It was Dafna.

"Hi, Dafna. It's Henny, from the ninth grade. How are you?"

"Oh! *Baruch Hashem*, I'm fine, thanks." Dafna sounded a little surprised to be hearing from Henny, but not unpleasantly so. "What can I do for you, Henny?"

Henny took a deep breath. She didn't think Dafna would be happier to hear what she was about to say than she was to say it.

"I don't think I'll be able to write for the newspaper anymore." The words came out in a rush. "I just wanted to let you know."

There was a long pause. Then Dafna asked slowly, "How come?"

Henny hadn't planned on telling Dafna why. It just wasn't the type of thing one shared — certainly not with a popular twelfth grader who was the editor of the school paper. But there was something about Dafna's tone of voice — the interest, the fact that she hadn't just given a knee-jerk reaction — that made Henny suddenly eager to talk.

She told Dafna everything. She told her about her earlier excitement when people told her how her stories affected them—and then about her encounters with Efrat and Gedalya. "And they're right," she finally concluded sadly. "It's like Efrat told me. I *am* writing my stories for other people. I might write about ideas and behaviors that are—I don't know, lofty—but I don't act that way myself!"

"So you think that to publish articles about these things is hypocritical?" asked Dafna.

Henny nodded, before remembering that Dafna couldn't see her over the phone. "Yeah," she replied. "That's it."

There was a short pause, and then Dafna seemed to totally change the topic. "Henny, think of your five favorite books."

"Huh? Why?"

"Just do it, and I'll tell you why."

It took Henny only a few seconds to compile a mental list of five favorite books. "Okay, I've thought of them."

"Fine. Who wrote them? I mean, what kind of people? You don't have to tell me their names."

"What kind of people?" Henny repeated. "I don't know. How should I? Four of them are ladies and one is a man ...."

"Do you think they're perfect?" Dafna asked.

"The books or the people?"

"Good question. I mean the people who wrote the books. Are they perfect?"

Henny thought. "I … I don't know. I mean, I guess not. Nobody is, right?"

There was such a long silence on the line that Henny knew that Dafna wanted her to think about what she'd just said.

"Do you think they always live by every single thing they write?" Dafna asked.

"Maybe not everything," Henny answered slowly, "but most of it."

"Still, there must be plenty of things they write about that they don't do themselves. Things they're probably still working on. Right? Would you rather they left out all those things?"

"I don't know. I guess not."

"You'd better guess not," Dafna answered. "Because a lot of people out there are still working on a lot of things. In every *middah*, every bit of behavior—everything!—there's room to keep growing. Just because you write about it, no matter how good your characters are—it doesn't mean you're there *yet*."

Henny considered that. "So then … what's a hypocrite?"

"A hypocrite," Dafna replied gently, "is somebody who thinks that the rules she applies to others don't apply to her. Someone who thinks that there's no reason to grow, because she's already there. And you're not that way. You're obviously working on yourself, or you would never have called me. I might be wrong, but this is the way I see things. A person has to be able to look in the mirror and see where she needs to grow. She has to look and see *herself*—not other people. A hypocrite sees where *other* people need to improve. Either she doesn't have a mirror, or her mirrors are wrong. They tell her she's perfect.

"Hashem has given you a gift, Henny, to be able to really talk to people through your stories, to help them grow and improve. If I were you, I wouldn't be so quick to give it up."

There was another long silence as Henny thought about what Dafna had said.

"You know …," Dafna added, "I remember the rabbi of my shul once getting up before giving a *mussar shmuess* and saying something like, 'Of course, I'm speaking to myself, too ….' Maybe you could do the same kind of thing by writing a short introduction to your stories, letting your readers know that you're working on yourself, too, and that the lessons in your stories apply equally to you."

"Wow …," Henny answered. "Thanks, Dafna. I guess I've got some things to think about."

As soon as she set down the phone, Henny walked to her dresser and picked up her mirror. She peered inside, looking at her face.

Yup, it was her. She had her faults and weaknesses—but she had strengths, too. And the biggest one was that she was still growing ….

Looking in the mirror, Henny gave herself a big smile.

ONE GOOD THING

When our afternoon teacher, Mrs. Rubin, announced that we each had to write an assignment about what we were best at and how we used our talents to contribute to the class, I was one of the boys who groaned.

I groaned super-loud, in fact, even though there was nothing particularly bad about the assignment. But I groaned about every writing assignment. Creative writing was no picnic for me; I know that it's not a picnic for any guy in the older elementary grades. For me, though, it was *really* not fun. That's because when I learned how to ride a bike, and play baseball, and even do math, the part of my brain that deals with reading and writing somehow got left behind. My tutor calls it a "language processing disorder."

Whatever *that* is. The bottom line is, I don't read or write the way a seventh grader is supposed to. I don't even read or write the way a fifth grader is supposed to.

As my parents keep drilling into me at every opportunity, I'm not stupid. I'm not even close to stupid. I just have to work a little harder at some things than my classmates do. But sometimes I feel pretty stupid. Like when the new teacher, who can't keep anybody's names straight and can't remember which kid in the class has a reading problem, called on me to read a horrendously long paragraph in the science book right in front of the whole class.

Or when the man in charge of the school *tzedakah* project came into the room and handed out registration papers for everyone to fill out so we could get our raffle booklets. Of course, everyone was excited about the campaign and the amazing prizes for those who sold the most tickets, but nobody remembered to ask me if I needed help. So there I was, slowly filling out my name and address as the other guys were jumping up and running to the front of the room to hand in their papers and collect their raffle books. When the man asked, "Is that it?" I was the only one to raise my hand slowly. I felt all the blood rush to my face.

Usually, though, life is pretty good. I've heard enough horror stories about kids with a problem like mine who were teased and bullied and pretty much tortured by their classmates, so I know that I'm lucky.

There are two reasons why my situation is better than most. Number one: I have a great class. We have good "group dynamics" or something like that. I picked that up from my mother when she came home from PTA last year. I'm good at remembering big words and figuring out what they mean. My tutor — he's really a special ed teacher, with special certification in working with the language arts, but I like to call him a tutor — says that since I don't read and write as well as other people, I listen better than they do. I think it's really true. I usually catch onto what the teacher wants for an assignment while the rest of the class is still saying "I don't get it" and "Huh, *what* do you want us to do?" That's another way in which I'm fortunate — some kids have problems processing language in both the spoken *and* written forms. I just have trouble making sense of printed letters. When somebody has a problem with processing spoken language, he can't make sense out of the words people are saying.

As I was saying, I'm in a good class, with nice, fun, solid boys, who don't need to pick on somebody to feel good about themselves. The second reason I'm fortunate: I have a talent. I can draw — not like most kids who think they can draw. I do really, really nice work. When I was four or five, my mother liked some of my pictures so much that she sent me to art lessons. I haven't stopped going since. I guess that whatever part of my brain confuses letters doesn't affect landscapes and objects.

My talent, I think, is what keeps me going to school with my head up and my pride intact. It's proof to the world that I'm not dumb, that all I have is a language disorder and the rest of me is working just fine.

Even after an embarrassing incident, I know that sooner or later a classmate will need me to draw something for him. Then it'll be, "Hey, Yerachmiel, help me out, will you?" If it's a class project, all twenty of my classmates will be saying that.

It's funny, but I notice that other kids are bothered when people ask for their help too often. Take Aharon, for example. He's the class brain. Every morning before a test, his desk is surrounded by kids asking for help. Usually he's patient, but sometimes, when the questions have been going on for ten minutes or more and he's getting bored of explaining the same line of *Rashi* for the fifteenth time, he starts to look a little irritated. Once in a while, he'll even say something like "Come on, you could figure that out yourself" or "Did you bother studying?"

I'm not like that. I don't know why, but it doesn't bother me when the other kids need help sketching or coloring or fixing up a project. Maybe it's because I myself need so much help with things that others take for granted, that it feels good to be on the giving end for a change.

It feels even better to be the class artist. For our creative writing assignment, it may have been hard for me to get my thoughts down on paper, but I had no trouble thinking of a subject. And art contests are the best. There's never been one that I didn't win—well, almost never. There was a contest last year that I nearly didn't win, though it was the most important one I've ever participated in. Let me tell you about that one.

"Boys, these binders are going to be something for you to keep, not just another school notebook to throw out at the end of the year." Our school had just launched a new *middos* project and the *rebbeim* were taking things pretty seriously. They'd just distributed new one-inch binders along with fancy, computerized worksheets and other handouts.

"We want you to be proud of this project, so we're going to hold a cover-designing contest. Every boy will design a cover, using whatever supplies he wants—markers, crayons, pens, pencils, paints. The covers are due in a week from today, and the teachers are going to choose a winner. Color copies will be made of the winning entry so that everyone can have one for the cover of their binders. Of course, you can use your own cover for your binder if you'd prefer."

As Rabbi Moskowitz introduced the contest, I began to sit straighter and straighter. This was something to take notice of! It wasn't that different from any of the other contests in which I'd participated over the years, but it would be fun just the same.

I felt a friendly jab in the small of my back. "Guess who's gonna win this one?" Mendy asked as he poked me with his eraser.

"Who — you?" I asked.

"That's right," he grinned back. Mendy's almost as famous for not being able to draw a straight line as he is for being the class winner in spelling bees. "You're just going to have to take second place this time, Yerachmiel."

Neither of us had any clue how close to true his words were.

I worked at that art project the way I always did: steadily and diligently. I was busier than ever. I'd come home from school, eat supper, walk over to study with my tutor and then go to shul to learn with my father and *daven* Maariv. After that I'd come home and go straight to my room, to work on the cover.

I'd decided to use paints, since they give the greatest range of feeling and texture to a picture. I drew small scenes depicting different *middos* in each corner of the paper, with the word "*Middos*" in the center, written in the fancy lettering that my art teacher had taught me. It was hard for me to learn lettering, but I plugged away at it. The lines and curves came easily to me, but I still had to figure out how to set up the letters to form words. That was the difficult part.

I had to show the pencil copy to my little sister, Michal, before I started painting, just to make sure that I'd spelled the word correctly. I didn't want any mistakes. This cover was going to decorate the binders of every kid in school.

On the morning that the binders were due, I got up extra early. I wanted to make sure that the cover was perfect and give myself some extra time if I decided it needed any touch-ups. I examined the paper from every angle, and finally placed it carefully in a brand-new folder, which I stuck in between two books in my knapsack. I didn't usually lug books to and from school since they were heavy, but I decided that the added weight was worth it. I wanted my project to be well protected.

The first indication that something was wrong — that things might turn out differently than expected — was the crowd of boys gathered around the table in the back of the classroom when I walked in. Looking more closely, I saw that all the covers were spread out on the table. It looked like everyone was hovering around one specific cover.

I put down my knapsack and unzipped it. I pulled out the folder and removed my own entry for the contest. Then I walked over to the table to see what everyone was looking at. I felt strangely nervous.

It took only a second to see what my classmates were so interested in. As I stared at it, my heart dropped. It was a picture — also done with paint, although in a very different style. I was pretty sure that it had been painted with watercolors. I'd used acrylics for mine. It was similar to mine in set-up as well, although there were plenty of differences. The workmanship and artistry that had gone into its production were masterful. Better than mine, I realized, with a sinking stomach and the bitter taste of defeat in my mouth.

"I didn't know that you could paint like this, Aharon," someone was saying admiringly.

"I didn't until recently," Aharon replied, flushed with pleasure at the compliment. "I just started art lessons last year. My art teacher helped me out, and I worked really hard at it."

"Hey, there's Yerachmiel!" Chaim said. "Let's see what he's got this time!"

Papers were pushed over hurriedly to make room for my cover in the center of the table, right next to Aharon's.

For the first time in my life, I felt slightly embarrassed as I set my picture down. It definitely wasn't as nice as

Aharon's. I barely saw the expressions of admiration that came over my classmates' faces as they examined it. All I could see was Aharon's beautiful watercolor, with its splashes of color and elegant design.

"This year we'll have a real contest," Mendy said cheerfully, nudging me playfully. "Usually it's just Yerachmiel against Yerachmiel, but now we have a second contender."

I smiled stiffly. The boys might not know the difference, but the teachers judging the pictures would. Aharon was going to win this one.

After politely walking the length of the table, pretending to examine each of the pictures in turn but seeing nothing, I headed back to my seat in a daze. I wished that I'd also thought to take my project to my art teacher on Sunday. He could have helped me polish it up, and maybe then it wouldn't have been all that different from Aharon's.

That wasn't my best day in school, to say the least. It was hard to concentrate on anything but the pictures lined up teasingly on the table in the back of the room. The classes passed by in agonizing slowness. When the bell rang to end the day, I was filled with a sense of relief.

"'Night, Yerachmiel," my friends said cheerfully as they passed me on their way out the door. They had no idea how I felt, so I forced a smile and watched them leave as I packed up slowly.

I was the last one in the room. I could hear the bus

motors running outside, but I was in no hurry to make the bus today. My house was close enough to walk, and I wanted time to be alone.

Before I left, I walked over to the table and stared down at the pictures—mine and Aharon's—lined up next to each other on the table. The teachers were going to judge them tomorrow morning, before class. We'd all know who the winner was as soon as class started.

I'm embarrassed to tell this over, but it's part of the story, so I'll say it anyway. As I stood there looking at Aharon's beautiful cover, ugly thoughts started to fill my mind. I wanted to ruin his picture. Different ways to do that paraded through my mind. I could rip it up into tiny pieces and throw them in the garbage. I could take Rabbi Moskowitz's thick black marker from the teacher's desk and scribble on it. I could simply crumple it up and toss it into the big garbage can next to the school's entrance, which got emptied every night into the green dumpster by the school gates.

I picked up Aharon's picture. No other cover on the table held a candle to my work. If Aharon's—the better one—was out of the running, I was the sure winner. I fingered the cover. He had used thin artist's paper, the same kind I'd used. The simplest action, a quick back-and-forth motion, would reduce the paper to nothing but colorful shreds. It would take only a second, and the room was empty.

Aharon would be disappointed, of course—but he'd live. After all, he was the class brain. The anger surged up in me again. What gave him the right to do this? He had everything—everything! The best mark on every test, *hasmadah* award every year in camp, a warm smile from the *rebbi* every time he opened his mouth in class …

And me? My talent was the one way in which I shone. It was the one thing that made me stand out, what made me feel good about myself. Aharon had taken all that away from me, just to get some more glory for himself and win another contest.

I listened closely and could hear nothing in the halls. The teachers were out by the buses now, and the janitor wouldn't be around for hours. Nobody knew I was still in the building. No one would ever know ….

I placed the picture down on the table and rushed to the door, reaching blindly for my knapsack. I couldn't trust myself to stay in that room for one more minute.

I didn't tell anybody at home about what had happened. It was too raw, too painful, and I'd come too close to doing something very wrong to want to discuss it. My mother asked me what was wrong, and so did my father. Even Michal asked me what was wrong! I just mumbled something about being tired.

I went to sleep early that night. I didn't have an art project to work on, and nothing else interested me.

The next morning, I arrived at school in the same mood as I'd left it the night before. Well, not quite. The anger had subsided somewhat and was replaced by a feeling that was closer to resignation. Resignation to failure. My talent, the one special thing that I'd always had, had been torn away from me.

"Hey, Yerachmiel, check out the board!" It was Naftali, pointing at the blackboard.

I glanced over without much interest. If the winners were posted, Aharon's name would be up there. Why would anyone be mean enough to point that out to the runner-up?

But Aharon's name wasn't up there under the bold heading of "Winner." Mine was.

It took me a long minute to process that fact, even as I smiled automatically while my friends slapped me on the back. I really was the winner. But—what about Aharon?

The pictures were still lined up in the back of the room. I went over to look at them as soon as I was able to separate myself from the boys gathered around me. It took me only a second to scan the table. Aharon's picture wasn't there.

The first feeling to hit me—interestingly enough—was guilt. I felt almost as if I'd actually ripped up Aharon's picture and disposed of it, as if I was the reason that he hadn't won. But I knew I hadn't done that. The next feeling I was aware of was curiosity. What *was* going on? Had somebody else been jealous of Aharon? And where was Aharon?

He was at his desk, reviewing yesterday's notes as usual, ignoring—purposely, I thought—the lively conversation about the contest. I walked over to him.

"What's going on?" I asked.

Aharon looked at me. "What?" he asked. "And by the way, congratulations! Your cover is terrific. I'm looking forward to seeing the color copies on everyone's binders." He sounded sincere.

I wouldn't be put off that quickly. "Thank you. But you know what I mean. What's going on? Where's your picture?"

"It's not there?" he asked. His face looked a little too blank.

"You know that it's not there," I responded. I knew what it was like to work hard on something, and I knew that if Aharon had said that he'd worked hard on that painting, he had. There was no way he didn't know that his picture hadn't been on the table that morning. "What happened to it?"

There was a long pause, and finally Aharon answered quietly, "I withdrew it from the contest."

"Why?" I asked. Had he done that out of pity for me?

The anger was surfacing again.

"Because it wouldn't have been fair," he answered after a pause. "I thought about it, and I realized that the cover wouldn't have come out so nice if I hadn't brought it to art class. Nobody else got help. You didn't."

"But I take art lessons. I wouldn't be so good at drawing if I didn't."

"Yeah, but there's a big difference between getting help with your skills by going to lessons and getting help with a project itself. It wouldn't have been fair." He shrugged. "That's all. Anyway, yours might have won. It's a really great picture."

I looked long and hard at Aharon. It was obvious that he meant every word he said.

"You know what?" I said. Aharon looked at me expectantly. "You're a real winner."

Aharon blushed. I moved back to my seat but my mind was whirling. I hadn't been joking when I told Aharon he was a winner. He'd done something big—something I knew I couldn't have done. He'd been honest with himself. He'd given up something that was important to him because he knew it was the right thing to do. And that made him a winner.

Suddenly, as I tried to wrap my mind around everything that had just happened, the term "winner" seemed to apply to me, too—for more reasons than just winning the contest. Life was full of struggles, and winning didn't mean that everyone had to know about it. I realized that I had so much going for me besides my artistic ability.

I try to do my best, even at the things I'm not so good at. I'm a good friend. I'm honest with myself. And I'm able — sometimes, at least — to stop myself from doing the wrong thing, even when it's very, very hard. I remembered standing alone in the classroom the day before, and I felt my guilt over so nearly giving in to temptation evaporate. I *hadn't* given in.

I have strengths, though they may not be visible to anyone else. They're just as real as any other strengths — maybe even more real.

Well, that's my story. I almost didn't win that contest, but I came out a winner in so many other ways.

GIVING UP

My older brother Yechezkel has a favorite story that he likes to tell about me. I was little when it happened, and I remember it so vaguely that I probably would have forgotten it long ago if Yechezkel didn't tell it so frequently.

It happened one day at a playground near our house. I was only three years old, and Yechezkel was watching me, as usual. I'm the youngest of eight children, so there were other siblings who could have taken me to the park. Somehow, though, it was always Yechezkel who ended up pushing me for long periods of time on the swing and waiting patiently at the bottom of the slide.

As we left the house that morning, Yechezkel says that my mother called after him, like always, "Make sure that the twins don't get too wild, and keep little Chani away from the monkey bars."

The twins were Moish and Uri. I was little Chani, of course. I didn't like being little or being called little. At least, that's what everyone tells me. I don't remember, but I'm proud that I had that much sense when I was only three.

There was nobody on the monkey bars that afternoon. That must have made them seem more noticeable to me than ever before. I remember standing at the edge of the playground and staring at those towering monkey bars, stretching way over my head. The sun was gleaming on every silver rung as if they had just been polished, and it seemed as if those monkey bars were just waiting to be conquered.

I knew that I wasn't allowed to go on the monkey bars. My mother reminded me every time I went to the park, but it must have suddenly seemed so unfair. After all, Miriam was allowed on the monkey bars. So were Moish and Uri! I wasn't so much littler than them; why, I was hardly little! Who said I couldn't handle the monkey bars? In the shimmering summer sun, they seemed to whisper enticingly, "You can do it."

Yechezkel says that he saw me looking at them. "Uh-uh, Chani," he told me. "You're too little for the monkey bars. Let's move away from here. Do you want to go on the swings or the slide first?"

Even at three, I guess I had that sixth sense that told me it would be futile to argue. As Yechezkel tells it, and as I remember, the next few minutes were spent calmly whooshing down the slide and being pushed on the swing. But the sunlight continued to sparkle on those monkey bars, and I could see them wherever I went — from the tippy-top of the slide and from my perch on the swing when Yechezkel pushed me high.

We had been in the park for about ten minutes when the inevitable happened. Moish and Uri began to act up. They had been digging quietly in the dry brown wood chips that covered the ground under the slide, but one of them must have annoyed the other. Suddenly, voices were raised and wood chips were flying, with a very real chance of somebody getting hurt if the fight wasn't broken up.

Yechezkel hurriedly lifted me off the swing and pushed me in the direction of the slides. "Go play on the slide for a minute," he told me, and rushed off to break up the wood-chip hurricane that was taking place nearby.

I headed toward the slide — and then stopped short. Those monkey bars had caught my eyes again, beckoning with all the allure of warm, shiny metal on a mild summer day. I changed direction and trotted off toward the monkey bars. I knew that I only had a minute or two. As soon as Yechezkel finished breaking up the fight, he'd come looking for me.

I was too little to feel guilty or scared about doing

something that wasn't allowed. From the moment I placed my foot on the first smooth bar, all I felt was the thrill of doing something new. Up, up, up I went, higher and higher, until the wood chips below me merged into a solid brown carpet. I gripped the bars tightly with my hands and looked across the playground, to where Yechezkel was still trying to separate the boys. I climbed a little higher. At that point, I was about halfway up the monkey bars and starting to feel slightly unsteady. I paused.

"Chani! No!" Yechezkel's shouts were urgent enough to distract Moish and Uri. The twins stopped fighting and stared. Yechezkel ran toward the monkey bars, and the two of them followed hot on his heels.

"Chani, what do you think you're doing?" Yechezkel yelled. "You know you're not allowed up there. Come down now!"

I hesitated.

"You're too little! You're gonna get hurt!"

That was all I needed to hear. I was *not* too little. No way. I reached for the next bar. The ground looked scary from so high up. But I wasn't going to give up, no matter what Yechezkel said.

"Chani, stop it right *now*! You can't do that!"

I climbed another rung, with my jaw set and teeth clenched. I could too do it. I was going to show all of them!

Yechezkel started up after me. I began to climb more hurriedly, to get away from him. I could hear him getting closer, but I was going to make it to the top — just to prove that I could. I looked back for a second to gauge my big brother's progress. Just as I reached for the last bar … I slipped.

It was a long fall to the ground. Of course, there were wood chips at the bottom and a rubber mat underneath them, but neither of those could protect me from the metal bar that came out to greet me as I fell.

Yechezkel says that he had never seen so much blood before that incident, and never has since then. I don't remember that part, but I do remember the bright lights of the emergency room and the huge doctor who spoke sternly to me before stitching up my chin.

"No more monkey bars, young lady," he'd said. I remember thinking defiantly that I *was* going to climb more monkey bars …. After all, why shouldn't I? I'd gotten all the way to the top that afternoon, hadn't I?

Like I said, Yechezkel still loves telling over that story. The funny thing was, the story didn't end there. It didn't end with the speech my mother gave Yechezkel about watching me more carefully in the playground, the one she gave the twins about behaving at the playground so that Yechezkel could watch me, or the one she gave me about never, ever, ever climbing on the monkey bars again — not till I was at least ten.

It didn't end because it was just the beginning. It was the beginning of my life as a girl who never gave up.

Part of it was the fact that I was the youngest in my family. By the time I was old enough to even think about riding a two-wheeler, all of my siblings had been doing it for years. I learned how to do it fast. I got up and fell down and then did it all over again—but I didn't give up.

When my mother noticed me squinting and brought me to the eye doctor, he looked at me in amazement. "Mrs. Fried," he said, "did you say she's been riding a *bike*?"

My mother nodded. "She's been riding without training wheels for a couple of months now."

The doctor shook his head slowly. "All I can say is that learning to ride a bike with this degree of nearsightedness must have been nearly impossible. Your little girl isn't a quitter, that's for sure."

My mother smiled. "That's true."

"Although," the doctor continued thoughtfully, "if she'd given up, we might have discovered this eye problem earlier …."

My mother nodded thoughtfully. "True," she said again.

When I started going to Sunday clubs in fifth grade, I decided to try out the origami club. The things they made were always so cute and original. Besides, my two closest friends, Dini and Sara Rochel, both wanted to join the origami club, too.

I was lost from the very beginning. I had never realized how many ways there were to fold a paper. I sat in the front row and tried to follow all the instructions, but I was so confused. I'd fold the paper the wrong way or miss a step, and all of a sudden I'd find myself holding a monstrosity that in no way resembled the shapes my friends were making.

I was so frustrated by the third week that Sara Rochel said to me, "Why don't you switch to a different club? I bet you'd love drama or the regular craft group."

"I can do this," I growled as I tried yet again to fold down the much-creased edge of lilac-colored craft paper to form the delicate leaf of a flower. It didn't look like a leaf at all. It looked more like my flower was sticking out its tongue at me.

But I was going to stick it out, because I wasn't a quitter. Someday, I'd come out of this with some passable origami.

And I did. It happened at the very end of the term, the last week of clubs, and it wasn't beautiful or anything. But it was passable. At least everybody could tell that it was a flower. I put that sorry, crinkled little five-petaled thing proudly on the edge of my desk. It was a mute and weathered testimony to the fact that I was no quitter.

I never gave up, no matter what. On the first day of school, my teachers would always mention our limitless potential and how we can do whatever it is we set our minds to, if we don't give up. I would nod knowingly as they spoke; I lived by that concept.

But I didn't know that my resolve was going to be tested.

The piano arrived at our house when I was twelve. Great-aunt Millie gave it to us when she moved down to Florida for the warmer weather. That was great for my older sister Adina, who'd been taking piano lessons for years and had wanted something better to practice on than our old Casio keyboard. Miriam was happy, too, since she'd always wanted to learn but had never had the patience to sit and plunk out scales on the keyboard. "The notes sound so real on this," she said happily, stroking the ivory keys of the old-new piano.

I had to admit that they did. When Adina played the same old songs that she tapped out on the Casio every night, they sounded so different. There was something special about playing on a real piano.

I wanted to play piano like my big sisters, and I told my parents as much.

"Ma, Ta, can I please take piano lessons along with Adina and Miriam?" I asked.

I saw my parents exchange a quick look. "The new piano is beautiful and I can understand that you want to learn how to play it," my mother answered slowly. "But Chani, you've never been that musical. Every time I asked you if you wanted to take lessons, you told me you didn't. And you know that you're better at art and writing …."

"Why does that mean I'm not musical?" I demanded. "Just because I'm good at art and writing doesn't mean that I can't play the piano."

"But you've never been in choir or anything …."

"Because I didn't want to be!" I answered. "I could have if I wanted to!"

"That's probably true," my mother said, nodding with resignation. "Are you sure you want to do this?"

I nodded. "Yes, I'm sure. And I'm *going* to do it, you'll see."

And I would. I was determined to do it, and nothing and nobody could stop me when I made up my mind to do something.

My family had to suffer through a lot of scales for the next two weeks. Scales don't usually sound all that bad, but with me plunking them out, they sure did. I could never seem to remember which note came next. They all looked and sounded pretty much the same to me.

The piano teacher, Mrs. Grunfeld, was very patient. She had me practice the scales again and again and again. I followed her instructions dutifully. I figured that as soon as we finished up with the scales and moved on to real songs, the notes would start to sound more like real music.

They didn't. It was a good thing that Mrs. Grunfeld believed in teaching her students to play piano "the real way," by learning to read music, rather than just playing by ear. Because both of us realized pretty quickly that an "A" sounded just like a "B" to me—and a "B" sounded almost exactly like a "C" or a "D." Sharps and flats were just words. I plunked out those notes again and again, trying to catch what it was Mrs. Grunfeld was talking about when she said enthusiastically, "Do you see, Chani? The B flat just sounds *flat*, doesn't it?" But it never sounded any different.

My sisters began to tease me. "Chani, could you play your scales for me again? Please? Pretty please?" Well, actually, only Miriam said that. Adina just smiled tolerantly at me. When she thought I wasn't looking as I diligently tapped out the scales, she slowly shook her head.

After six weeks of lessons, Mrs. Grunfeld asked for a conference with my mother and me. "I don't think we're getting anywhere with Chani's lessons," my teacher said frankly. "And it's not for lack of trying," she added quickly, as I opened my mouth to interrupt. "Quite the contrary, in fact. Chani is one of the most diligent students I've ever taught, but … I just haven't seen any progress."

Before my mother had a chance to say anything, I burst out, "But it's only been six weeks! These things take time — that's what everyone says! Adina's been taking lessons for six *years*, and she's still learning!"

Mrs. Grunfeld nodded patiently. "There are some things that may take six years or much longer to learn, but there are other things that should be learned in days or weeks if a person has any sort of aptitude for music. That's what I'm talking about."

"But I can do it!" I said stubbornly. "I *know* I can. I just need a little more time."

Slowly, Mrs. Grunfeld continued, "However, I certainly don't mind trying some more. It can't hurt, and there's always a chance of improvement, I suppose." She looked at my mother. "I just thought I should let you know about the status quo, so that you could decide whether or not you want Chani to continue."

I was all but jumping up and down in my chair at that point. "Please, Ma, I can do it. I just need a few more weeks and you'll see. I don't want to give up yet."

Mrs. Grunfeld looked at my mother. "It's up to you, Mrs. Fried."

My mother looked at me and nodded slowly. "I

suppose we can continue for another couple of weeks and see what happens."

"Chani certainly isn't a quitter," Mrs. Grunfeld said fondly, smiling at me.

"No, not at all," my mother agreed, but there was something about the way she said it that almost made it sound like a bad thing.

About a week after that conversation with my mother and Mrs. Grunfeld, my cousin Nechie came to visit.

Nechie was my age, but I hardly ever saw her, since she lived in Eretz Yisrael and tickets were so expensive. Her family was here now for a family *chasunah*, and they came straight to our house from the airport.

The first thing my cousin Nechie did, after saying "hello" and depositing her luggage upstairs, was spy our piano. "Wow, a piano!" was the second thing she said. Within seconds, she had seated herself on the piano bench and was playing. She didn't play like me, or even like Adina. She played almost professionally, with her fingers skimming the keys and her whole body swaying along with the music. It was almost like the music was *inside* her.

It made me burn to practice more, so that maybe one day I could do what she was doing.

"Do you play?" Nechie asked suddenly, as she finished the song.

"Uh … not really, yet. I've just started and I'm still on scales," I admitted.

"Oh. Well, I'm sure you'll learn quickly enough, if you practice a lot and you have the talent."

I looked around to make sure nobody else was listening, and then said, "Let's say you practice a lot and don't have the talent. What then?"

Nechie laughed. "Then you look for a different hobby. What's the problem?" I was staring at her as if she'd sprouted a second head. How could she speak about giving up on something so casually, as if she was discussing a change in menu for supper? "Really, I went through that myself."

"Through what?" I asked, feeling curious despite myself.

"I ended lessons for something I wasn't good at, and looked for something better. That's how I got started on piano."

"What did you take lessons in before?" I asked. I couldn't imagine Nechie doing anything in her free time besides playing the piano. It just seemed so much a part of her.

"Art," Nechie answered. "And I was terrible at it."

"But maybe if you'd tried for longer …," I began.

"Then I would have been miserable for longer," Nechie

finished. "Trust me, to become really good at something you have a talent for is hard enough. Why try to do something that you don't have a talent for?"

I looked at Nechie, and then at the piano. I thought hard … and I thought about painting. I'd always been good at art. Maybe Nechie was right and it was time to try out something new—like giving up for a change.

"Ma," I said the next evening, "I've decided to give up on the piano. I think Mrs. Grunfeld is right. It's really not going anywhere."

My mother stared at me, and then broke into a big smile. "That sounds like a good idea, Chani. Is there anything you'd like to try instead?"

"Well … I was thinking about art lessons, if you don't mind," I began. "Maybe just a four-week trial?"

My mother's smile grew wider. "That sounds fine, Chani," she said. "Just fine."

TOUGH KID

When Chezky got back his test, he didn't squirm or blush or even bat an eyelash when he saw the big red seventy-five that graced the top right-hand corner. It wasn't that he didn't care, and it wasn't that he hadn't studied. He had studied, actually—for a couple of hours with his tutor, several with his father and a few more grueling ones on his own.

It was just that Chezky was a tough kid. He was never scared or worried, or anything like that. There was no way he was going to get upset over a test mark. He had a reputation to live up to.

"Mendel Ellinson," Rabbi Berg said, handing back a test paper to a thin boy in the front row. He accepted it with his right hand while nervously pushing his glasses up his narrow nose with his left. "A perfect one-hundred, I might add." He smiled down at Mendel, who blushed.

Mendel lived right up the block from Chezky. His family had moved in a year earlier. Except for the requisite polite questions and comments in the days and weeks after Mendel had joined the class, the two had barely spoken.

Chezky didn't scowl, though, as Mendel stared bashfully down at his paper. He was tough. It wouldn't do to be upset or jealous over another boy's grades. No, that was for other kids—not the tough ones. Chezky could handle anything.

On the playground, too, Chezky was known as being tough. He was really, really tough sometimes. In fact, as soon as he showed up with his classmates, the younger kids occupying the basketball court grabbed their ball and scampered away. No one wanted to mess with Chezky.

Don't think that Chezky was a bully. He wasn't. He never shoved or threatened another boy, and he certainly never hit or punched anyone. But he was big and strong and tough-looking, so when he said, "It's our turn to get the field now," no one wanted to contradict him.

That afternoon during recess, Chezky acted as tough as ever.

"What did you get on the test, Moish?" Eli asked. Eli and Moish were Chezky's good friends, and the three of them were walking across the playground together, slightly ahead of the rest of the class.

"Ninety. What about you?"

"Eighty-seven. And you, Chezky?"

Shmulie, another classmate walking nearby, sighed at the question. "C'mon, guys, don't be so nosy. Didn't Rebbi once tell us that it's not nice to compare grades? You might make someone feel bad."

Chezky bristled at Shmulie's comment. Why did he have to say that? He didn't need any help, and definitely not from a soft kid like Shmulie. But before Chezky could comment, Eli laughed.

"Oh, come on. Chezky doesn't care. Right, Chezky?"

"Yeah, Chezky's tough." Moish sounded admiring. "Anyway, what did you get?" he asked curiously. The question was friendly. Moish and Eli knew just how long Chezky had studied for this test.

"Seventy-five," Chezky answered casually, in the same tone of voice his friends had used to describe their grades. Why should he mind that Eli asked? Only babies cared about marks. Not tough kids like him …

It was during sports that Chezky really shone. It didn't matter what the sport was—basketball, baseball, hockey or ping-pong. As long as there was a ball and sneakers involved, Chezky was happy. He was able to hit balls the farthest and shoot the most baskets. While his toughness didn't help his test scores, it certainly got him places in sports. When he stepped up to the plate, whoever was playing pitcher on the opposing team took a giant step back. When he held the big orange ball during a heated basketball game, hardly anyone tried to wrest it away from him.

It wasn't that Chezky didn't play fair. He did. But he was so big and tough — and such a good player — that nobody felt like getting on his bad side, even during a game.

Chezky loved to play. He was outside every recess — even in the cold of winter, amidst flurries and drizzles. As long as he could get somebody to play with him, he played. After school, too, Chezky played in the park until it got dark. If it was pouring outside or too cold, he slammed the ball across the ping-pong table in the basement with a friend or one of his brothers. If there was no one around to play with him, he hopped on his bike and pedaled furiously around the neighborhood.

When he was in action, Chezky felt strong. He felt big, fearless and important. Nothing and no one could bother him. He was tough in every sense of the word.

That changed somewhat when Chezky was in seventh grade. It all began on one bright spring Sunday in the park ....

Chezky and most of his classmates had gotten together for a baseball game. The weather was so beautiful that it seemed a shame to waste it indoors, even to those less inclined to play sports. The game was proceeding like any other. The weather seemed to have given them all some extra energy, too. The ball seemed to have taken on a life of its own as it was pitched and swatted and fielded so quickly that it seemed almost like a blur.

Chezky was, as usual, at the center of it all. He was the pitcher for his team, and his pitches were controlled and fast. On any other day, those pitches would have been enough to guarantee his team a quick win. But plenty of other boys were playing well, too, and as ball after ball was hit, it was all Chezky's teammates could do to prevent the other team from scoring.

Chezky was batting well, too. The first time he stepped up to bat, he sent the ball whizzing into left field to allow two of his teammates to come home. He got more hits in his second and third times at bat, and at the fourth try, he really sent the ball for a trip.

That was in the eighth inning, when the game was almost over. He calmly watched the ball sail over the heads of the outfielders and beyond the fence at the edge of the park before he set off on a jog around the bases. He reached home plate just as Shaya Cohen, who was playing center field, yelled, "The ball's lost … I can't find it in all these bushes!"

That was serious business, since they were playing with Avrumy Neustein's new ball. Avrumy's grandfather had brought him that ball on his last visit and it couldn't be lost. They *had* to find it. Chezky sauntered off the field along with his teammates to search the underbrush around the park fence. There were plenty of low bushes and tall grass growing on uneven ground that made good hiding places for a ball.

Chezky began to comb through a group of bushes that were a couple of hundred feet away from second base — just where he thought he'd seen the ball disappear. He worked slowly and carefully, since the bushes were dense and sometimes thorny.

Bending down on his hands and knees and peering under a bush, Chezky suddenly saw two things. The first was the ball, resting on a soft patch of green grass, as if it was waiting to be found. The second was a nest of dried grass and twigs. In the middle of the nest were several tiny brown creatures. Mice? Chezky leaned closer. No, they weren't mice. Their little ears, still pressed tightly against their heads, were longish … Rabbits! He counted them. There were five baby rabbits, and they were the smallest ones Chezky had ever seen.

"Any luck?" Shaya called. It sounded to Chezky as if he was a hundred miles away. He felt like it was just him and those tiny, helpless creatures ... and the ball.

"Yeah, I've got it," he heard himself shout back.

What were the baby rabbits doing there? Chezky didn't see a mother rabbit anywhere. Had they been abandoned? He reached out one hand and gently stroked the nearest rabbit. It was velvety soft and covered with fine brown hair. It opened up its mouth silently, as if it was asking for help.

"Chezky? Where are you? What's going on?"

"I'll be there in a minute," Chezky answered. He couldn't tear his eyes away from the baby rabbits. They each had a white spot on their faces, and their eyes were still tightly shut. They had the tiniest, most perfect toes on each foot.

Shaya came over to investigate. "Hello, what're you waiting for? You've got the ball, so what's —" He suddenly caught sight of the baby rabbits and fell silent. "Cool," he said in a hushed whisper.

"Chezky? Shaya? Guys, we've only got one inning left. Let's go." Moish was walking over purposefully, hands on his hips, like an umpire who feels a game has been interrupted for too long.

"Where's my ball?" Avrumy asked anxiously. The rest of their classmates were tramping through the brush to see what was happening.

"Here's the ball," Shaya said, picking it up and tossing it to Avrumy. "Chezky found it ... and look what else he found!"

"Hey, bunny rabbits!" exclaimed Reuven, a short, chubby boy with glasses. He stretched out a hand to pick one up.

Chezky grabbed it. "Don't," he said. "You could hurt it."

"The mother might not come back if you touch them," spoke up a quiet, measured voice. "That's why you're never supposed to touch baby animals. Usually, the mother is around, just waiting for people to leave. But sometimes she won't come back if she smells that a person touched one of the babies." It was Mendel speaking.

Chezky was surprised that his shy, studious neighbor knew so much about animals. But before he could think about that, he was hit by worry.

"I touched one of them," he told Mendel. "Just a tiny touch with the tip of my finger. Do you think it'll make a difference?"

"I don't know," Mendel answered. "We can wait and see."

"Why don't we finish the game and then come back and check?" Shaya suggested.

Chezky agreed, but his mind wasn't on the game. It was on the tiny rabbits under the bush, way back behind second base. What if the mother never came back? What would happen to them?

He couldn't wait for the game to end so he could check on them. To his teammates' chagrin, he struck out during his next turn at bat. He simply wasn't concentrating.

When the game was finally over, Chezky hurried right back to the bush. Mendel was close behind him. "Maybe we shouldn't all go," Mendel suggested gently to his classmates. "We don't want to scare away the mother if she came back."

The other boys were disappointed. They all wanted to see the baby rabbits again and find out what happened. But Mendel seemed to know what he was talking about, and when Mendel spoke up, he was almost always right. The boys reluctantly headed back home. Only Chezky and Mendel remained.

They reached the bush and bent down to look. There were the baby rabbits — without a mother.

"Let's move away a little, where we can't be seen from here," Mendel suggested. "We can watch and see if the mother comes back."

It was a good idea. They waited and waited. It was weird for Chezky to sit there alone with Mendel. They were neighbors and had barely exchanged a word all year, and now they were sitting together on the grass in silence, with only the sounds of birds and crickets in the background. An hour went by before Mendel said, "It doesn't look like she's coming back, does it?"

Chezky shook his head sadly. "What now?"

"Now we can take them home. We can run over to those stores across the street and get a box to put them in. Then we'll ask my neighbor, Mr. Kramer, what to do. Mr. Kramer knows everything about animals. He once worked in a zoo, and another time in a nature reserve."

That sounded like a good plan of action to Chezky—except for one thing. He wasn't sure about the "we" business.

"I can keep them in my house," he asserted. "My mother doesn't mind these things." He wasn't too sure about the truth of that statement, but he figured that he could always sneak the box up to his room. What his mother didn't know wouldn't hurt her. He didn't want Mendel to bring the rabbits over to his house and keep them all for himself.

He didn't have to worry. Mendel grinned. "That's good, because my mother is really, really scared of animals."

Mr. Kramer was not happy to see the rabbits. "Why'd you take them home?" he asked.

"We waited for the mother and she didn't come back," Mendel answered. "We thought that since somebody touched the rabbits, maybe she wouldn't be back again."

"Well, she's not going to come back while you're sitting there. She can smell you, even if you think you're well hidden. Mother rabbits will always come back."

Mr. Kramer sighed in exasperation. "Boys," he muttered under his breath.

"Uh … what can we do now?" Chezky asked uncomfortably.

"Well, we'll have to take care of them." He looked sharply at the boys. "Are you up to waking up every four hours to feed them?"

"Every *four hours*?" Chezky gasped.

Mendel gulped.

"That's right. Baby animals burn energy very quickly, because they need the food to grow and develop. And besides for feeding, they need warm bedding, like straw or wood chips, and a warm place in the house to sleep. It can't be drafty. Their bedding will have to be changed once a day. Are you up to this?"

Chezky looked at Mendel and Mendel looked at Chezky.

"We can't just put them back now, I guess?" Mendel asked weakly.

Mr. Kramer shook his head. "By now the mother has probably given up looking for her babies. She knows where she left them and if they're not there, she'll assume they were eaten."

Chezky felt horrible. That poor mother rabbit …

Mendel heaved a deep sigh when they left Mr. Kramer's house. "You're sure you can bring them home?" he asked.

"Do I have a choice?" Chezky responded. He gingerly held the box with the rabbits. They were moving around a lot now and kept opening their mouths as if they were asking for food. Mr. Kramer had said that meant they were hungry. Chezky couldn't blame them. It must have been hours since they were last fed.

"I'll help," Mendel offered. "Let's go to your house to make them some milk, okay?" Mr. Kramer had told them what to add to regular milk so that it would be healthy for the baby rabbits.

The boys set off together with the rabbits. It no longer seemed strange to Chezky to be working with Mendel. They were on a mission together, and that was all that mattered at the moment.

Thus began a long few weeks for Chezky. His schedule revolved around the rabbits. He set his alarm clock for the middle of the night so he could feed them at three in the morning. To make sure they were fed often enough, he had to stay up until eleven at night for the late night feeding and wake up at seven for the morning feeding. There was no more oversleeping and coming late to school!

The two feedings that had to take place during school hours were the most difficult to arrange. Chezky's little sister Malky offered to do the afternoon feeding, but what about the morning one?

"Feed your rabbits?" Chezky's mother asked nervously. "Chezky, I don't even like having them in the house! You want me to *touch* them?"

"Please, Ma? I called up Rebbi last night and he said that he prefers I don't take them to school ...."

"Well, I guess I can understand that. All right, Chezky, I'll try. But next time, please leave the baby rabbits where they're supposed to be!"

"Okay, Ma, I know that now. But I thought they were going to die there. I couldn't just leave them!"

Mendel came over to help with the late afternoon feedings, but it was Chezky who bore the brunt of the work. For the first time, there were some days when he had no time to play outside in the afternoons.

"No, sorry," he told Shaya on the phone one day. "I have to feed the rabbits, and then I have to learn with my father and do my chores, and then I have to feed the rabbits again."

He really cared about those rabbits. There was something so delicate about them, from the soft folds of their ears to the tiny fingernails at the end of each toe to the startling red of their little mouths when they opened them to suck milk from the syringe. They were so dependent ....

One night, his mother stood in the doorway and

watched as Chezky fed the rabbits. He was so totally focused on his task that he didn't even notice her. She watched the way he tenderly cradled one bunny in his left hand while squeezing a drop of milk out of the syringe with his other. His forehead was furrowed in concentration.

Chezky didn't look very tough at that moment.

The rabbits grew bigger. They opened their eyes and learned to stand up. Soon Chezky didn't have to wake up in the middle of the night to feed them anymore. Then they stopped needing milk altogether and switched to a diet of rabbit food and vegetables.

That was when Chezky's mother told him to start looking for homes for them. "You can keep one," she said. "Only one."

Which one, Chezky wondered, as he arranged for four of the rabbits to be adopted. He'd already given them all names ….

The episode with the rabbits was over so quickly that it almost seemed as if it had never happened. Chezky gave away four rabbits and was left with one furry brown bunny in a brand-new hutch in the backyard. Now the rabbit just had to be fed and taken out to be played with once a day, which Chezky did with much enjoyment.

His life was almost back to normal, even with his new pet. Chezky wasn't, though. He didn't realize that until he found himself walking to school one day with Mendel.

They'd started walking to school together when the rabbits were tiny. Most mornings, Mendel was at Chezky's house at seven o'clock to help feed the babies so they could both get to school on time. Afterwards, it only made sense for them to walk together. Even when the morning feeding was no longer necessary, they kept it up. After all, they only lived a few houses away from each other.

That morning, they rounded a corner near their school, and Chezky stopped short. A little boy was walking toward them, sniffling. Chezky almost didn't notice him. He wasn't bawling or waiting for someone to help, but he was definitely crying a little.

"What's the matter?" he asked gently, approaching the little boy. He noticed how he towered over the kid, and bent down quickly so that he was at eye level. "Do you need help?"

The little boy shook his head. "You can't help," he said, voice quivering.

"Try me," Chezky said persuasively. "Maybe I can't, but tell me what happened anyway."

The kid starting crying in earnest. "My ... my father gave me a dollar to buy a treat because I got a hundred on a test yesterday. And I lost it! It fell out of my pocket.

Now I can't get a treat, and I don't have any snack …."
He sniffled.

Chezky dug into his pocket. He came up with a quarter, a dime and three nickels. Fifty cents. "You have any change?" he asked Mendel.

Mendel found a quarter, a dime, and a whole lot of pennies. He handed them to Chezky, who poured all the change into the little boy's hand. "That's almost a dollar," he told him. "Think that'll help?"

The little boy looked up at him with wonder. "Yeah … thanks!" He was off like a rocket toward the small kosher grocery store they had just passed, hands clenched tightly over the change.

Chezky looked at Mendel and grinned. "That worked."

Mendel nodded. He looked thoughtful. "You know something?" he said suddenly. "You're not so tough anymore."

Chezky looked startled. "Huh?"

"You're not so tough anymore, like you used to be. People aren't scared of you anymore."

"Scared of me?" Chezky stared. "I never scared anybody!"

"You scared me, all right," Mendel told him, coloring slightly. "Right when we moved in. You were so big and strong, and you talked like you owned the block. I was scared to even try and make friends …."

"Really?" Chezky asked. He'd always seen himself as tough, but definitely not scary.

"Yeah, but you're not like that anymore. I don't know why ... unless it was the rabbits."

They walked the rest of the way to school in silence. Chezky thought about what Mendel had said. He knew his friend was right; it *had* been the rabbits. They'd opened him up to seeing a new part of himself—a gentle, thoughtful, caring side.

Chezky took a good, hard look at himself, and found that he liked what he saw much better than what had been there before. And from the way Mendel was looking at him as Chezky absentmindedly held the door open for his new friend, it was something that other people liked better, too.

THE SCARY HOUSE

The tall dingy-white house at the end of the street had always seemed somewhat mysterious, but it only became downright scary the summer that Chaya Raizy turned ten. That was the summer when, during an enthusiastic—well, perhaps over-enthusiastic—game of Machanayim, Chaya Raizy's friend Esther threw the ball so hard that it flew straight over Shira Neustein's head, out of Chaya Raizy's yard, across the narrow street and against the window of the tall white house. The window didn't break. The girls were sure of it. But when Chaya Raizy, Esther and Bina tiptoed across the lawn to retrieve the ball, the front door flew open.

Mrs. Pilchik, the skinny old lady who lived in the

ancient, tumbledown house, stood in the doorway wearing an old, faded housedress. She planted one hand firmly on her bony hip while she squeezed the doorframe with the other, as if she might just give a push and bring the whole house tumbling down on the three hapless girls cowering in the bushes only ten feet away. Her white hair stuck out in wild strands from her head, and her lips were pursed tightly together.

Most frightening of all was her silence; she didn't say a word. She just stood in the doorway and glared fiercely. Her gray eyes looked like two hard shiny pebbles, and they were practically shooting sparks through her steely gray glasses. Chaya Raizy had a feeling that if they stayed there one more minute, all three of them were going to be burned up alive by those sparks.

Chaya Raizy grabbed Esther with one hand and Bina with the other. "Let's go," she squeaked.

The three girls fled across the street and into the safety of Chaya Raizy's house. Their other friends followed them inside and listened with avid interest as Chaya Raizy described what had occurred.

"Wow," Toby finally breathed, when Chaya Raizy finished describing how frightened they had been and how fortunate they were to have made it back across the street. "Scary!"

The other girls nodded silently.

"We didn't say sorry," Esther commented regretfully.

"You're joking, right?" Chaya Raizy responded indignantly. "We hardly got out of there alive!"

Shira looked upset. "You didn't get my ball, after all that?" she asked.

"Are you nuts?" Bina retorted.

"I just told you—we barely made it out of there with our *lives*!" Chaya Raizy gasped dramatically.

Shira looked unconvinced. "That was my new Machanayim ball. My mother got it for me because I babysat my little sisters for two nights in a row last week." She heaved a sigh. "Well, maybe I'll go pick it up on my way home."

"You'd better not," Chaya Raizy told her. "I'm not gonna be responsible for whatever happens to you!"

Shira just snorted, but she didn't cross Mrs. Pilchik's lawn that afternoon to get it. She claimed that she didn't want to trespass, but Chaya Raizy knew the truth. She was plain old scared, just like everybody else.

After that day, the tall white house became known as "the scary house." The girls seldom saw the old lady, but they could easily imagine her standing at the window and staring long and hard at them every time they walked down the block. The house gave them a deliciously spooked-out sort of feeling. Chaya Raizy got shivers up and down her spine just from *looking* at it.

Chaya Raizy's brothers laughed whenever she spoke about the scary house. They said she was a scaredy-cat.

Her parents said that Mrs. Pilchik wasn't really scary, or even mean, but just a lonely old lady who'd had a hard life. They said she was a nice woman, if you just got to know her, and that there was nothing all that scary about her house.

When Chaya Raizy's little sister Adina turned five and started walking home from the bus stop on the corner by herself every afternoon, Chaya Raizy welcomed the opportunity to teach her the truth. After all, Adina would believe her.

"You need to stay far away from that house," she said ominously, nodding seriously at little Adina's solemn expression.

"Really? Why?" Adina squealed.

"There are scary things there." Of course, Chaya Raizy didn't totally believe that. But it paid to exaggerate a little, if it meant that defenseless little Adina would be more careful. "Stay far away, sweetie, okay? You never know what could happen to you in a scary house like that …." Adina shivered and cuddled up close to Chaya Raizy, who felt big and loving and protective.

Every day, Adina jumped off the school bus and ran down the block as fast as she could, her long pigtails streaming behind her and her knapsack bouncing up and down on her back. She didn't look to the right or to the left until she finally reached her gate and flew up the walk, relief flooding her little body.

She fell into her seat at the kitchen table, gasping, as she allowed the warm homey smells of supper cooking to fill her with a sense of security and love.

"Why are you so out of breath, Adina?" her mother asked with concern. "You don't have to run all the way home from the bus stop, you know."

Adina didn't answer. She *did* have to, but her mother wouldn't understand. Whenever Chaya Raizy mentioned the house on the corner, her parents responded sternly that we shouldn't judge people or talk badly about them.

No, it was better that they didn't know how scared she felt …. But it was so scary to jump off the bus every day and run down the block with her eyes focused on the welcoming sight of her own little gate, never turning to look at the rickety old house as she passed.

So Adina never told anyone. No one — not even Chaya Raizy — would ever have found out just how scared she was if it wasn't for one bitterly cold day in late fall, during the first snowfall of the year.

Everyone commented that it was early for snow — too early. But the weather was just right for snow, with a biting wind and a flock of heavy clouds, and snow it did.

School had started as usual that morning, but by early afternoon, the principal of Adina's school decided that the girls should be sent home as quickly as possible. Snowflakes were falling fast and furious, and the snow was sticking tight to every surface. Roads and sidewalks and rooftops were quickly being blanketed by white, and the younger children would have trouble walking if it got any deeper.

The class mothers rushed through their lists to ensure that a parent or older sibling would be home to greet the children when they came home. At Adina's house, her older brother Motty answered the phone. He was home with a bad stomachache that had slowly disappeared as the day wore on. His mother called it a 24-hour virus. Motty was feeling pretty much back to himself and was quite bored.

"Hi, is this the Adler residence?"

Motty answered in the affirmative.

"Adina is getting dismissed early today because of the snow. Is there someone who can be home to meet her when she comes off the bus in half an hour?"

"Sure," Motty responded. What other plans did he have at the moment?

Adina was boarding the bus with her kindergarten friends at about the same time as Motty's friend Shea got home from school. The first thing he did was call Motty.

"Hey, Motty, guess what? And by the way, how are you?"

Motty grinned. "What? And I'm much better by now,

baruch Hashem …. I just had enough of a bug to miss a day of school. Perfect, huh? Anyway, what're you doing home from school already?" He could see Shea's home number on caller ID.

"That's what I wanted to tell you! Mr. Epstein was out sick today and they didn't bother getting us a sub, since we'd probably get out early anyway because of the snow. So we just got out super early. How great is that?"

"Really great," Motty answered, even as he felt a stab of regret. Couldn't they have been dismissed early on a day when he was in school?

"Anyway, wanna come over? The snow is perfect for building a fort. My older brothers will be home soon and I want to get a head start on them."

Motty had been stuck inside the house all day, and one glance out the living room window told him that the conditions outside were every bit as exciting as Shea reported. "Coming!" was all he said as he jumped up eagerly from the couch. Motty threw on his coat, grabbed his boots and was out the door faster than you could say "snow fort." As usual, he locked the door behind him conscientiously.

Fifteen minutes later, his little sister came walking slowly down the block, watching as her shoes — she hadn't brought boots to school, since her mother hadn't heard the weather forecast before sending her off that morning — formed little drifts in the snow as she walked.

Adina loved the snow. It looked so fresh and white and inviting. More inviting than the snow, though, was the hot cocoa that she knew her mother would have waiting for her. That, and the warm soup bubbling on the stove, ready for supper. Adina shivered a little and tried to quicken her steps, but it was hard. The snow was growing thicker, and her toes were starting to feel a little numb.

Adina reached the front door of her home and sniffed. Sometimes, she could smell the hot cocoa even from outside. She couldn't smell it today, but that didn't matter. Soon she'd be sitting at the table, smelling — and tasting — the real thing from up close.

Adina reached for the doorknob and turned it — or rather, she tried to turn it. It didn't budge. She tried again, and then realized that her mittens made it too hard to get a good grip on the handle. She pulled off one mitten and turned the knob again, but it still wouldn't turn. The door was locked. That made sense. Somebody had probably locked it on his way out, not realizing that she'd be coming home. She knocked on the door. No answer. Adina knocked again, more urgently this time. The only response was the softly falling snow that was blanketing the ground more heavily than ever.

Adina stared up at the big empty windows of her house. Where was everyone? Her teacher had said that every single mommy had been called. There was supposed to be somebody home in every house. She lifted both hands and banged on the door as hard as she could. Then she stood back and waited. Nothing happened. Adina started to cry.

The back door was always locked, but Adina trailed around the house to make sure. It was locked. After that, she had no more ideas. She walked back to the front yard, the tears trickling down her cheeks, where they threatened to freeze into little icicles. She knew that her friend Malky lived somewhere close by, but she wasn't sure exactly how to get there by herself. The thought of being lost in an unfamiliar neighborhood with the snow falling all around scared her more than anything. At least here she knew where she was.

Her knapsack was beginning to feel very heavy. Adina dropped it into the snow next to her door. She sat down on the top step and shivered. There were no *frum* neighbors on her block, nobody that she could rely on if she needed help. There was an older couple next door who were always polite and friendly, but they had a big black dog. Adina was terrified of dogs, especially big black ones.

Adina sat there, and continued to sit, as the minutes ticked by and her hands and feet began to feel like solid blocks of ice. She was beginning to feel somewhat warm and cozy bundled up inside her coat. The snow began to cover her shoulders, and her eyelids started to close. Suddenly, there was a tap on her shoulder. Adina blinked drowsily up at the tall figure standing over her, and then drew back in alarm.

It was old Mrs. Pilchik from next door! Adina shivered in fear. She stood up and tried to run, but she was too numb, and she stumbled and fell right in front of her own door. She lay there, unable to move, waiting for Mrs. Pilchik to grab her with her long, claw-like fingernails.

When the hand came, it was surprisingly gentle, though insistent. "Get up, little girl," said a raspy voice. "Get up right now or you'll freeze solid out here."

Adina didn't want to freeze solid, but she didn't want to go anywhere with Mrs. Pilchik, either. She stared at the old lady and was startled to see that her gray eyes appeared warm and concerned. Mrs. Pilchik stretched out a hand and Adina took it. She needed help from *somebody*, and Mrs. Pilchik was the one offering it.

Adina expected the house across the street to be dreary, dimly lit and drafty, but it wasn't. It was surprisingly cheerful, with a log fire crackling in the fireplace and paintings on all the walls. The first thing Mrs. Pilchik did was to take off Adina's shoes and tuck the little girl under a blanket on the couch. Adina couldn't stop shivering. Then Mrs. Pilchik went to the kitchen and boiled a cup of water on the stove, in an ancient-looking teapot. She poured the water into a Styrofoam cup, on top of a teabag. She added lemon juice and honey, and gave the cup to Adina to drink.

Adina hesitated. Was tea kosher? Mrs. Pilchik saw her hesitation and smiled. "Look," she said. She showed Adina the box of tea, the jar of honey and the bottle of lemon juice. She pointed to the *hechsher* on each of them. "It's kosher," she said. "Drink up."

Little Adina needed no more convincing. She drank up, and the hot, sweet tea filled her with delicious warmth. Mrs. Pilchik disappeared into the kitchen again and came back a minute later with an unopened package of cookies, which she presented to Adina, again pointing out the *hechsher*. Adina smiled and took one.

Motty was in the middle of building a huge snow fort when he suddenly remembered something. It popped into his head as though it had been waiting for him to remember it, and his face turned almost as white as the snow.

"Oh, no!" he gasped. "My little sister!" Without another word of explanation, he tore down the street.

Adina wasn't in front of the house. Motty had no idea where to look next. He glanced around desperately. Just then Chaya Raizy came down the block.

"Chaya Raizy!" he called wildly. "Adina's missing!"

"Missing?" she responded blankly. "In this weather? How's that?"

Motty explained briefly what had happened. Chaya

Raizy wasted no time on accusations. She stood there and thought, and then she quickly unlocked the front door and started to check one room of the house after the next. She checked the garage and the shed, and then she felt as lost as Adina had felt a short while ago.

She opened the front door and looked into the bushes to make sure Adina wasn't there. The front door of the house across the street opened and old Mrs. Pilchik looked out. "I have your sister over here," she called.

Chaya Raizy's jaw dropped. There? In Mrs. Pilchik's house? And she was expected to go inside, too?

Well, she couldn't leave her little sister alone — certainly not *there*. Bravely, Chaya Raizy ran across the street.

From up close, Mrs. Pilchik didn't look all that scary. She was tall and skinny, and she was wearing a long, faded housedress — it might have even been the same one she'd been wearing when Chaya Raizy had first met her in the summer. But her face was surprisingly gentle, and she didn't sound mean at all when she told Chaya Raizy to come in.

There, on the couch, was Adina. She looked warm and cozy and very much at home. "Adina!" Chaya Raizy exclaimed. "We were so worried about you!"

Adina's face lit up when she saw Chaya Raizy. "Nobody was home," she said in a little voice as Chaya Raizy sat down next to her on the couch and gave her a hug. "Nobody answered the door."

"It was a mistake," Chaya Raizy told her. "A big mistake. But now everything's okay, sweetie, right?"

Adina nodded.

"Thanks to you," Chaya Raizy said suddenly, turning to Mrs. Pilchik, who'd been standing and watching in silence. "I don't know what would have happened otherwise … Thank you."

Mrs. Pilchik smiled, and suddenly Chaya Raizy had absolutely no idea why she'd ever thought that the old lady looked scary.

"Maybe you'll come back?" Mrs. Pilchik asked the two girls quietly. "I like visitors. And I keep a kosher kitchen …."

"Really?" Chaya Raizy said.

"Yes, and I have lots of interesting things I could show you, too."

Adina's eyes brightened. "Could we, Chaya Raizy? Please?"

Chaya Raizy smiled slowly. "You know what, Adina? I don't see why not." She gave Mrs. Pilchik a big smile. "Thanks again," she said. "I'm going to tell my mother what happened, and she'll probably want to come over herself to say thank you."

Mrs. Pilchik smiled. "Just tell her that the biggest thank you she can give me is to let her beautiful daughters come over and visit."

The girls waved as they walked through the front door and left the "scary" house behind them forever. They'd be back the next evening—but this time they knew the house was nice and interesting, and filled with love and friendship.

COUNT ON IT

"So, what are we doing for Mommy and Tatty's anniversary?" Tammy was talking, and her voice was beginning to take on a note of impatience. Their parents' anniversary was coming up in just five days, and she still hadn't managed to get her siblings to sit down and decide how they would celebrate. Tonight, their parents were at a wedding, and they had a good, long supper time to make plans — if everybody cooperated.

"Well, a party, I guess," Dina volunteered.

"We'll have balloons, streamers — that sort of stuff, won't we?" Donny asked.

"What about a present?" Tammy asked.

"Earrings?" Aviva asked. There was a chorus of

restrained giggles. Aviva was five, and had been promised earrings for her sixth birthday, which was coming up in just two months. It felt to Aviva as if she'd been waiting to get pierced ears forever. Aviva thought and talked and practically breathed earrings these days ....

"I don't think so," Tammy vetoed the idea gently. "We want something that will be a nice present for Mommy *and* Tatty. I can't exactly picture Tatty walking around wearing a pair of earrings, huh?" At the new chorus of giggles, Tammy continued sternly, "But it's great that you came up with an idea, Aviva. Does anyone else have one?"

At this, everyone sobered up again.

Baruch sighed. "It's so hard to think," he complained.

Tammy shot him an exasperated look. "Baruch, you always—"

Just then Donny suggested, "How about a new coffee table or something? You know, a piece of furniture?"

"But we got a coffee table last year," Dina countered. "Remember, Tante Sossie gave us the one from her basement that's almost as good as new? I don't think Mommy or Tatty really want a new one just yet."

"How about a new *bentcher* holder?" That was Yanky's idea. "Our old one broke a few weeks ago, and it was all scratched up, anyway. I think Mommy and Tatty got that for a wedding present."

There was a chorus of agreement at this idea. Tammy

looked relieved. "Is that settled, then? We'll get a *bentcher* holder?"

Everyone nodded.

"I have a *chavrusa* in fifteen minutes," Yanky announced. "Is that it?" He was already halfway out of his chair.

"No!" Tammy exclaimed. "We have to decide who's in charge of which jobs. And what should we serve?"

"How about lasagna?" Dina suggested. "I know how to make it!"

"Okay, so you'll take care of that, then."

Dina nodded enthusiastically. "And I'll make a salad to go with it." She'd recently graduated from cooking simple recipes to more complicated ones, and had made lasagna for supper one night. She happily welcomed the idea of making a special batch for her parents' anniversary supper.

"I'll pick up the present, but I need all of you to give me five dollars toward it tonight," Tammy continued. Everyone nodded again. "I'll also bake the cake."

"I'll decorate it!" Aviva said excitedly, bouncing up and down.

"Okay," Tammy agreed. "Now, I need volunteers to buy soda, get streamers and balloons, decorate the dining room, make a card …" Tammy's forehead creased, as if she was trying to think of what they had missed. "I think that's it," she finally said. "So, who's doing what?"

"I'll make the card," Donny suggested. "I can use the new pencil set that Zeidy bought me for my birthday."

"I'll buy the soda on the way home from yeshivah," Yanky offered.

"Okay ... that just leaves the actual decorations."

"I'll do that," Baruch offered.

A sudden, uncomfortable silence filled the room. Baruch's siblings looked at each other for an instant, then looked away.

But Tammy quickly recovered. "That's okay, Baruch. I think I'll just take care of the decorations myself."

"Okay ..." Baruch said, slowly. "So what should I do?"

Yanky jumped in. "We don't have to decide every last detail right now, Tammy," he said, meeting his sister's eyes intently.

"Fine," said Baruch, grinning, "but don't forget to give me a job, too. I'll see you guys later!" Baruch got up from the table and headed outside.

A minute later, Yanky caught up with Baruch in the backyard and pulled him aside.

"Baruch," Yanky said quietly, "I didn't think it was right to discuss this in front of everybody, but there is something we need to talk about."

"Yeah, what is it?" Baruch said, eyebrows raised suspiciously.

"Well," said Yanky carefully, "the reason Tammy didn't want to let you handle the decorations for the party is that … well, sometimes you seem to have a little problem with, uh … following through. You know, you say that you'll do a job—and I'm sure you really mean to do it—but in the end, it doesn't get done."

Baruch crossed his arms over his chest defiantly. "I don't know what you're talking about."

"Baruch, I'm not trying to make you feel bad. But, seriously. Don't you remember this past Sukkos, when it came to putting up the light in the *sukkah*? You said you would take care of it before *erev yom tov*, but you never did. Guess who actually hung it up, ten minutes before candle lighting?"

"That wasn't my fault. Nobody reminded me!"

"You're not supposed to need reminders to take care of something you agreed to do. And what about this past Sunday, when you said you were going to rake the leaves?"

"That was different. I had a big game with my friends! We'd been planning it for weeks, and Mommy said I could go!"

"*Mm-hmm* …" said Yanky, unimpressed. "And what about the poem that you agreed to write for Bubby's birthday party? It ended up being all of four lines long, because you first started working on it about half an hour *after* the party began. Do you see what I mean?"

"That's not tr—"

"Look," Yanky interrupted. "I'm telling you, as your

older brother—this is something you need to think about." He paused. "Do you still want to take care of the decorations?"

"Yes, I do," answered Baruch, glaring at at his brother as if daring him to say anything more. "And don't worry—I'll get it done."

"Okay, then. It's yours. Just don't mess it up."

Baruch marched upstairs to his bedroom, kicked the door closed and flopped down on his bed, fuming. *What do they think I am, a three-year-old? They think I can't get anything done?*

But then, through his anger, memories began to surface against his will. His little sisters coming to him with broken toys, and his earnest promises to fix them ... Sitting in the basement at Bubby's house as the joyous sounds of partying were going on above him, scribbling away desperately on a scrap of paper trying to produce a passable poem that was due to be presented in just five minutes ... Proudly assuring his father that he could hang up the *sukkah* light on his own this year ... Agreeing to rake the leaves and then remembering about the big ball game ... And lots of other times, too. Lots of times when he'd really meant to get the job done, and done on time—but somehow, it just hadn't happened.

Baruch sat up suddenly. Well, this time it was going to happen. He was going to show them, and he was going to show himself, too. He could meet a deadline; he could get things done. The house would be decorated beauti-fully for his parents' anniversary. And it would all be due to his own hard work and responsibility.

He hurried over to his desk and grabbed a piece of loose-leaf paper from the nearest binder. Hunching over it, Baruch started to write a list of everything he'd need. He'd go to the store tomorrow to pick up the decorations, before any of them even started to work on their own jobs. He would show them!

Baruch was true to his word, although it was raining heavily and Avigdor invited him over along with a bunch of friends after school to try out the new computer game he'd received for his birthday.

"I wish I could come," he told his friend regretfully, "but … I have something else to take care of."

Off he trekked, into the biting wind and stinging raindrops. It was truly an unfriendly evening. Now that night was falling so early, it was hard to leave school and find the streets already dark—and doubly hard to take care of errands on his way home, knowing that a nice, warm supper awaited him in his own cozy kitchen.

But Baruch went straight to the store, which was sev-eral long, wet blocks out of his way. Once there, he care-fully selected some brightly colored balloons, matching streamers and even a big sign that read "Congratulations!" When he was back outside, he headed down the block and toward his house. He finally arrived home, half an hour later than usual, cold and wet.

His sister Tammy met him at the front door. Silently, she gripped his wrist and led him upstairs, where he found all of his siblings already assembled in the girls' bedroom.

"Change of plans," Tammy hissed. "Zeidy has a cold. Bubby suggested that we make the party at their house. That way it'll be easier on Zeidy, and it will also be much easier to set up and to get Tatty and Mommy to the party without them knowing about it. Okay, everyone?"

Everyone was more than okay with the idea.

"But we're going to have to make the party early, because Bubby and Zeidy go to sleep early. It's a good thing that the anniversary falls out on Sunday."

"What time?" Yanky asked.

"I was thinking that six o'clock would be a good time," Tammy answered. "That gives you and Baruch enough time to get home from yeshivah and get ready."

"I'll probably drop off the sodas tomorrow afternoon on my way home," Yanky commented. "That way I won't be in such a rush on Sunday."

Tammy nodded and consulted her notepad. "Dina, the two of us can do the cooking in Bubby's kitchen on Sunday afternoon. That way, Mommy won't suspect anything."

Dina agreed eagerly. There was something exciting and special about using Bubby's kitchen.

"Okay," Tammy said finally. "Committee dismissed."

Baruch got up slowly. This changed his plans a little. He'd hoped to have plenty of time to hang up his decorations on Sunday evening before the party. He wouldn't have too much time if the party was so early.

"Hi, Bubby?" he spoke into the phone a minute later. He glanced surreptitiously at the door to his father's study. His father let them use the study phone when he wasn't home, but all he needed was for one of his parents to walk in on him now. "How's Zeidy feeling? … Better? … Oh, good. Anyway, I was wondering if I could set up for the anniversary party on *motzaei Shabbos*? … No? … Oh, you're having a parlor meeting then? Wow, Bubby, do you need any help? … Okay, yeah, Sunday will be fine. Thanks, Bubby. … I love you, too. Bye!"

Baruch frowned as he hung up the phone. Bubby was chairwoman of a *tzedakah* organization in their community, and every year she hosted a parlor meeting in her dining room to raise money. Just his luck that it was taking place that week!

Well, Baruch figured, he'd just have to be super-organized and go to Bubby's house right after school was over on Sunday. He was still going to prove to his siblings that he could do anything he put his mind to — and do it right.

As Baruch entered his room, he saw Yanky bending over the bags next to his bed.

"What're you doing?" Baruch asked.

"Oh, just looking at your decorations," Yanky replied. He started to walk toward the door, then stopped and turned to look at Baruch. "I like them, by the way. You picked out good ones."

"Thanks," Baruch answered.

"Gonna have everything ready on time?" Yanky asked.

For some reason, this time Baruch didn't get angry. He turned to face his older brother. "That's right," he answered. "You can count on it."

Somehow, as he left the room, Yanky found himself believing his younger brother. There was something about the set of his jaw and his steady tone of voice that told Yanky he could be counted on.

Baruch had planned to bring the decorations to school with him on Sunday so that he could walk over to his grandparents' house straight from school. But on Sunday, the weather was even worse than it had been the previous week. Raindrops were pelting down relentlessly, and the sidewalks were flooded.

The decorations made it all the way to the front door, when Baruch looked out at the soaking wet day and hesitated. He hurried back up to his room. He'd have to come home to pick them up after school. It didn't pay to take the chance of dropping the decorations into a mud puddle and ruining them.

Baruch found himself hurrying home from school mid-afternoon. He would have plenty of time to decorate Bubby and Zeidy's dining room, to be sure, but he wanted everything to be perfect, and perfection takes time.

Baruch rushed into his house. He made a quick stop in the kitchen to take a drink and saw a note on the table from his mother stating that she'd gone shopping and would be home much later, after stopping in to visit Bubby and Zeidy at six o'clock. Baruch smiled to himself. Their ruse had worked. Apparently, Bubby had asked Mommy to drop in.

Nobody else was home, which made sense. Yanky had mentioned that he was planning to go over to his friend's house after school to study for a test and was going straight to the party after. Donny was out with their mother, and the three girls were already at Bubby and Zeidy's house.

In a minute the house would be totally empty. Baruch ran up to his room to grab the decorations. He made a quick stop in the bathroom and—

That's when it happened.

Baruch turned to leave the bathroom and reached for the doorknob. It was stuck. Stuck? Whoever heard of a bathroom door being stuck? Well, it happened sometimes in stories, but this wasn't a story. This was real life, and the bathroom door in his house was—*stuck*!

He rattled the doorknob but it wouldn't budge. He threw his weight against the door and wiggled the doorknob again. Still no luck. Baruch stepped back and took a deep breath. Then he attacked the door again, pounding the top banging the bottom, and rattling the knob over and over again. It was no use. He was stuck, a prisoner in his own bathroom.

Baruch sat down on the edge of the bathtub and considered his options. He very quickly came to the conclusion that he didn't have any. The bathroom was on the second floor, and there were no tree branches or anything like that rising up to the window, like there always are in books. There was nobody home, and Baruch had absolutely no way out of the bathroom.

It wasn't fun to be stuck. There wasn't much Baruch could do in the bathroom, and he was bored. But worst of all was the thought of the decorations that he'd picked out so carefully, sitting in the bags right outside the door. Would they ever get to the party? Would Baruch himself get to the party?

Baruch rested his head in his arms and waited … and waited … and waited.

The preparations were coming along nicely in Bubby's house. The lasagna was just about ready to go into the oven, and the cake was ready to be iced. The sodas were chilled, and the dining room table was set.

"The party starts in a little less than two hours," Tammy commented. "I hope Baruch leaves enough time for putting up the decorations."

Dina sighed.

Half an hour later, Tammy looked at her watch. She was letting Aviva decorate the cake, and her sister was doing a surprisingly good job. With nothing to do, Tammy worried about the passing time.

"I wonder where Baruch is," she said fretfully. "He said he'd be here right after school. Let me call home."

She called from her grandparents' phone and listened as it rang again and again, until the answering machine finally picked up.

"No answer," she said at last.

As Dina slipped the pan of lasagna into the oven and Aviva gently poked another chocolate lentil into the frosting on the cake, Tammy walked over to the window and looked out. All she saw was rain. "That Baruch," she muttered to herself. "I should have known …."

The minutes ticked by. Dina folded napkins into pretty fans, and Aviva pushed the decorated cake to the back of the counter. Then Yanky showed up.

"Where's Baruch?" he asked immediately.

Tammy gave him a sour look. "I can't believe this!" she said irritably. "Even if he shows up now, it'll be too late to do a nice job. And I wanted everything to be perfect …."

Yanky's reaction was different, though. "It's strange that he's not here …," he said, looking disturbed. "I know he's been working hard on this. He went out and bought the decorations right away. He had them all ready to go when he got home from school. In fact, I really think he's changed in the past few days." It took him just a few seconds to make up his mind. "I don't like this — I'm going home to check on him."

The house was quiet, and Yanky felt suddenly nervous. Could something have happened to his younger brother? He proceeded cautiously from room to room and almost jumped out of his skin when he heard the rattling coming from upstairs. He followed the sound up to the bathroom.

"Hey!" he shouted. "Baruch?"

"Yeah! I'm stuck!" The call was only slightly muffled by the door.

It took a screwdriver and five short minutes before the boys were standing face to face.

"How'd that happen, anyway?" gasped Yanky, short

of breath from the exertion involved in removing the doorknob and forcing the door open.

"Dunno," Baruch responded. "But we'd better run! I have to put up those decorations."

"Do you think you can still do it in time?"

Baruch looked at him with the new expression that Yanky was getting used to.

"I don't know, Yanky, but I'm gonna try. You can count on it!"

As they charged outside into the rain, Yanky decided, despite the past, that he would do exactly that.

THROWING IN THE TOWEL

Ariella scowled at her open math notebook. She'd been working on an algebra problem for five minutes already and had finally come up with an answer. The problem was that she was relatively certain that the answer she'd reached was not the correct one. The idea of starting fresh, of turning to a new page in the notebook and writing out the problem *again*, and figuring out *another* answer, was extremely unappealing.

Ariella stood up and called her friend Debby to discuss the scarf and glove set that her mother had bought her that day in the mall. She had picked the blue one, but now she thought maybe she should have taken the pink ....

A fifteen-minute discussion left her feeling more

settled. Yes, the blue was the right choice. She'd really known that all along.

She went downstairs to the kitchen, picked out a bag of Super Hot and Wild spicy potato chips from the snack cabinet, poured herself a cup of apple juice, and sat down for a leisurely snack at the table while her three-year-old twin brothers steered matchbox cars around the legs of her chair in hot pursuit of each other. When she was finished eating, Ariella sat down to read a chapter of the book she'd just taken out from the library — at least she told herself it would only be one chapter.

"Ariella," her mother said, entering the living room, "did you finish your homework yet?"

"Almost," Ariella answered, glancing up from the book. Wow, was she up to page eighteen already? "I just have a few math problems to finish up."

"Your bedtime is an hour away," her mother reminded her firmly. "Please go upstairs and finish your homework. If you have extra time, you can continue reading."

Ariella sighed deeply, but she put down the book without argument. She hopped back up the stairs and into her bedroom. The math problem looked even less inviting now than it had looked an hour ago. Ariella gritted her teeth and settled down in front of the notebook. She decided to skip ahead to the next problem and see if it was any easier.

It wasn't. This time she didn't even manage to come

up with an incorrect answer. She had a page full of lines and numbers—and, well, no solution. She thought about calling up Mimi, who was great at math, for help, but decided against it. It would be too hard to follow along with Mimi over the phone. To learn math, you had to be sitting with the person teaching it and watching as she figured it out.

Should she ask her father for help? He was an accountant, but accountants didn't use algebra, did they? Ariella remembered, when she was little, asking her father what you needed to do to become an accountant. Her father had smiled and tousled her hair.

"Oh, not much," he'd said. "You just need a lot of school. And you have to be good at adding and subtracting." He hadn't mentioned algebra, so why should Ariella expect him to remember this stuff from eighth grade?

She had four questions left. Halfheartedly, Ariella tackled the third problem, and promptly got stuck. Her efforts on the last one were even more halfhearted—and rushed, too. Ariella figured that if she wasn't going to accomplish any math, she might as well get back to her book as soon as possible. The plot was really shaping up to be interesting ….

When her mother knocked on the door to her bedroom fifteen minutes later, she found Ariella all ready for bed and cuddled up with the book.

"Is your homework done?"

"Yup," Ariella answered. "I had a hard time with some of the math questions and I don't know how well I did."

Her mother nodded with a yawn. "Well, it's the effort that counts, right? I'm sure your teacher will be satisfied."

Ariella herself wasn't so sure, but didn't think it was wise to discuss the matter further. She just nodded and smiled widely. "Good night, Ma."

"Good night, Ariella," her mother said, before shutting the door softly.

Ariella gave one more uneasy thought to the math problems in her notebook that were all but buried by haphazard, careless scribbles and wrong answers before the story pushed all thoughts of algebra out of her head with a big, comfortable shove.

When she put down her book that night and said Shema, she fell asleep right away.

Ariella came home from school the next day with a countenance that was a lot less serene than it had been the night before. She stomped into the house.

"What's the matter, Ariella?" her mother called from the living room. She knew from the sounds Ariella was making that something was wrong.

"Nothing," Ariella called back gloomily. After all,

what could she say? She hadn't told her mother the night before about the true state of her math homework—not really. So how could she explain what her math teacher had said? That her work showed a lack of effort? That she was irresponsible? That the teacher expected improvement within the next week or she'd have to call Ariella's parents?

No, none of that would sound very good. But maybe … was there something else she could say? Something that would help her get out of this situation once and for all? The wheels started to churn in Ariella's head even as she set down her knapsack next to her bed.

By the time Ariella came downstairs for supper, she was looking her usual cheerful self. Her mother smiled as Ariella walked into the kitchen. "Glad to see you looking happier than when you came in," she commented.

Ariella just smiled back. Then she sniffed appreciatively and said, "Supper smells great, Ma." Her mother always appreciated compliments about her cooking. Besides, the food that was bubbling on the stove really did smell good. Or maybe the nervous butterflies that had accompanied her home had disappeared and left behind a ravenous hunger.

She'd already come up with a good plan. She'd wait to talk to her parents until her father came home and had some time to eat supper and relax from a day of work. Then she'd begin a short, nice conversation with her parents ….

At first, things proceeded right on track. Ariella and her siblings finished eating. Ariella helped out by clearing off the table and earned some grateful praise from her mother. Her father walked in the door at six o'clock, right on time. He left his briefcase on the floor next to the door and hung up his coat and hat neatly on their hooks. Then he walked into the kitchen for supper.

Ariella waited for her father to finish his soup and begin the main course before walking into the kitchen. She was gratified to see him look up with a smile. "Hi, Ariella. How was your day?"

"Great, *baruch Hashem*," she answered. "School's going really well this year. I'm working hard and really learning a lot." She noticed her father's smile grow wider. Effort in schoolwork and living up to one's potential were sore points between Ariella and her father.

"But," Ariella continued, "I'm having a little trouble—with math." She noticed her parents exchange a rapid glance. Ariella had an uneasy feeling that her mother had just figured out the true reason behind her cheery and helpful attitude that evening. "I just don't seem to be catching on."

"As I remember it," her father said evenly, pausing to take another bite of chicken, "you were begging to be registered for the advanced math class this year. That was just a few months ago, you know."

Maybe this wasn't going to be as easy as she'd thought.

"Well, yeah," she conceded, "but that was only because Debby was going to be in the advanced class. Now that I see it's not working out—"

"*Hmm*," her father inserted. "I don't remember that. I seem to remember you talking about really liking math and wanting to turn over a new leaf and try hard."

"Well, that, too. I mean, I did like math—last year. And I really have been trying. It's just that … I can't do it." Ariella assumed a most woebegone expression. "I had four examples to do for homework last night. Really long and tough ones. And I did all of them! But I got all of them wrong—every single one!"

"You could have asked me for help. You can always do that."

"I know, but I … I thought that accountants don't use algebra, and you learned it so long ago that, well, maybe you'd forgotten it."

Her father chuckled, but it wasn't with as much humor as Ariella would have hoped. "As a matter of fact, accountants do use one or two algebraic principles now and then. And no, I don't think I've forgotten all of my elementary school math just yet."

"Oh," Ariella said in a small voice.

"And even if I had, you certainly could have asked."

"Well, uh … next time I'll do that. But in any case, I was just wondering if maybe—"

"You could switch to the easier track?"

Ariella nodded eagerly. "Right. I think it would be better for me in the long run. You know, keep my grades up so I can get into a good seminary."

Ariella's father regarded her long and steadily. She was sure he was about to say yes, to agree with her that this was the most sensible solution. But he just shook his head slowly and asked, "So you're throwing in the towel, just like that?"

Ariella stared back blankly. "Huh? What towel?"

"Throwing in the towel means to give up. To just decide that you're not good at it anyway ... so why keep trying? And it seems to me that what you want to do fits very nicely into the category of throwing in the towel."

"But I did try!" Ariella defended herself. "I tried hard! I'm just not that good at it. And anyway, it's not like I'm dropping out of math or anything. I just want to move to the ... the ..." She searched for the right word; she didn't want to say *easier*. "... less difficult track. You did that for Shevy when she was in eighth grade! She was also in the really hard high school-level algebra class, and you let her switch into the other track. I remember!"

"Well, there were differences between you and Shevy," her father countered patiently. "Do you want to hear them?"

Ariella frowned and shrugged.

"Well, whether or not you want to, I will tell you anyway. You *did* bring up the subject, and once you're comparing, I want you to realize why the comparison doesn't work." Her father continued to hold her eyes with his steady gaze. "There is the issue with effort in school-work. Shevy tries as hard as she can in all subjects, and she did so in eighth grade as well. Shevy is a straight-A student. And," Ariella's father was looking at her sternly now, "that's not really because of any difference in abil-ity. I believe that you are every bit as capable as Shevy, which brings us to the second point I want to mention. Shevy has a hard time with math. She wasn't sure if she wanted to be in the harder track for math. Her seventh-grade teacher recommended it because her math grades had always been so good — but the teacher didn't realize how much effort it had taken Shevy to get those marks all along."

"And you, Ariella … you wanted to be in this class. You asked for this challenge. I don't think it's far enough into the year to know whether or not you've failed to meet it yet. How many tests have you had so far?"

"One," Ariella answered sullenly.

"And your mark on that test?"

"Eighty-two."

"Right. Definitely not enough of a reason to switch classes in the middle of the year. And I have a feeling that you can get a ninety on the next one if you just put some more effort into it."

With that, her father returned to eating his dinner.

After a moment, though, he sat up straight again and turned to address her.

"And Ariella," he said, "once we're discussing this, do you remember the clarinet lessons you started last year?"

Ariella nodded slowly. Yes, she did.

"Do you remember why they stopped?"

Ariella thought. The lessons had lasted for only a couple of months, but she couldn't quite remember *why* they'd stopped. She did remember the intense longing she'd had to play an instrument, and the way that dream had died away very quickly and been replaced by the sheer monotony of playing one long, boring scale after the next.

"They stopped because you asked us to stop them. It was taking too long to see progress and you didn't want to invest the necessary time and effort." He paused for a moment to let the words sink in. "Do you remember the jewelry-making kit that Bubby bought you last year for Chanukah?"

Ariella nodded again. She did remember, vaguely.

"What happened to it?"

"I think ... I think Esty has it."

"That's right. And Esty is turning out some pretty impressive pieces of jewelry. But you were the one who requested it. Why aren't you making jewelry?"

"Um ..."

"You aren't making jewelry," her father said, "because

a certain one of your siblings laughed at your first attempt. So you simply decided that you weren't good at it and that making jewelry wasn't for you." Her father paused for a minute. "Do you see what I'm getting at?"

"I think so."

"You have a habit of throwing in the towel any time something gets a bit too hard or uncomfortable. You don't like to work when you don't see success immediately and clearly, right in front of you. That's a problem. In life, most things don't come so easily. And generally speaking, success isn't always that clear either. Sometimes, you can work for hours and days, and the only success you see is that things haven't gotten worse. And that," her father said seriously, "is what life is all about: working hard and doing your best and not giving up, no matter what—even if it's hard."

Ariella watched her father's plate absentmindedly. The rest of the chicken must be cold already. Her father smiled at her. "Just think about it a little, Ariella. And let's make a deal about the math. When's your next test?"

"In two weeks."

"So how's this? If you show effort—and I mean real, intense effort—for the next two weeks, and you get an eighty or below on that test, we'll consider switching your track."

Ariella nodded. Two weeks was a long time, but then

she'd be free. "Thanks, Daddy." She left the kitchen without the lightness of heart she'd hoped for, but with a feeling that at least relief was not too far away in the distant future.

There were four math problems for homework again. She'd hoped that after speaking to her parents she wouldn't have to do them, but … She took out her notebook with a sigh.

At first, homework proceeded the same as it had the night before. She got the first question right — or at least, she got an answer that she felt *could* possibly be right. And she got the remaining three so confused that she no longer had any idea what she was up to when she was only halfway through.

But that night's session ended differently than the one before. After all, Ariella had pledged to put in effort …. So she called Mimi.

It was hard to work over the phone, but Mimi was patient. After fifteen long minutes on the phone, it occurred to a grumpy Ariella that Mimi was really being nice. The time was going by just as slowly for Mimi as it was for Ariella — and Mimi wasn't even getting anything out of it.

They got through two of the three troublesome

examples when Mimi said, "Oh, Ariella, my mother needs the phone. Do you think you can do the rest on your own?"

"Yes," Ariella answered. "And thanks a million." She thought she was okay—or at least more okay than when she'd started. She now had a little bit of a better idea what to do with this crazy math.

But the fourth example didn't go easily. Ariella wanted to give up, but she'd promised to try, so try she did. After three separate starts and no solution, she took the problem to her father. Twenty minutes later, her homework was done.

Ariella looked at the clock, horrified. A whole hour had gone by—an hour wasted on math homework!

There would be only two more weeks of this, she consoled herself. Only two more weeks.

The next day, Ariella did something she'd never really done before during math class. She paid attention. Good, close attention. For one thing, she actually hoped for once that the teacher would call on her to read an answer from the homework. Let her see how much work Ariella was putting in. And for another thing, she didn't want to waste an hour of her time on math homework the next night, not if she could help it.

That night, math homework only took her forty minutes—and she got two answers right without any help.

Two days later, the strangest thing happened during history class. Ariella found herself taking notes. She blinked down in surprise at the neat lines in her notebook. That was weird. She'd started paying attention in math and had somehow forgotten to stop when math ended and history began.

Well, Ariella figured, she might as well continue taking notes, since class was half over anyway, and the truth was … it was actually pretty interesting.

One week after Ariella's conversation with her father, she managed to do her math homework in half an hour, with no snacks or other breaks—and with no outside help at all. Ariella felt the strangest feeling of satisfaction as she closed her math book gently and gazed down at the neatly printed figures filling the page of her notebook.

Just three days before the two-week deadline, the strangest thing occurred. Ariella's math teacher called her over after class.

"Ariella," she said, "first of all, I want to let you know how much I appreciate the improvement you've been showing throughout the past … *hmm*, it must be almost two weeks now since I've noticed the difference."

Ariella found herself blushing. She didn't know what to say.

"I wanted to ask you to help out someone else. Hindy is having some trouble with what we're learning now, and I know you live in her neighborhood. Do you think you might be able to study with her for the next test?"

Ariella heard herself answering "Okay," even as she yelled at herself, *Now you'll have to study good and hard for this test! No way you'll get below an eighty!* But what else could she tell her teacher?

As she was leaving the room, Ariella realized that she didn't care anymore. She was—dare she admit it to herself?—*happy* that she was doing better, and happy to stay in the class.

Her mother was surprised, later that week, to find Ariella sitting cross-legged on her younger sister Esty's bed, carefully stringing tiny beads onto a string to make a bracelet. It was coming out okay, but not like Esty's. Not yet. But Ariella—and her mother—had a feeling that just a week or two of honest effort could change all that.

Ariella's father wasn't surprised at all when, a month later, Ariella approached him. "Uh, Daddy? Do you think, maybe, that I could try out the clarinet lessons again?"

And no one was surprised when, six months later, Ariella was asked to play clarinet for the school concert. Least of all, Ariella herself.

THE TWENTY-THOUSAND DOLLAR QUESTION

A twenty-dollar bill. It was crisp and straight and green. And it was all my own. I fingered it happily. It might sound funny, considering the fact that I'd just turned twelve, but it was the first time I'd ever owned one.

Not that my family was poor or anything, *baruch Hashem*, and my grandparents were plenty generous. But the gifts I'd always received for birthdays and other special occasions were just that—gifts, not money. They were beautiful gifts, ones that had been picked out with thought and care, and I loved them. Money wasn't usually handed out in my family. None of my relatives seemed to think that a ten- or eleven- or twelve-year-old boy needed any money of his own.

On Chanukah I got *gelt*, and sometimes it added up nicely. I might have made more than twenty dollars this year, in fact, but it was in bits and pieces. Zeidy and Bubby had given me ten dollars, and my father had given me a dollar each night, and I had received fives from two or three different uncles. I'd never added it all up and traded it for a twenty, because most of the money from the beginning of Chanukah was already spent by the time the end of Chanukah came around.

So this was a first, and it was special. Zeidy had given it to me on *motzaei Shabbos*, as the music was playing and relatives were coming and going, and I was beginning to think that everybody had forgotten about me.

It was kind of funny to feel that way, because it was my birthday. But that's what happens when you share a birthday with a twin sister. Chani had become *bas mitzvah* and was basking in everyone's attention, praise and presents, while I might as well have been part of the wallpaper for all the notice anybody gave me.

It was dumb for me to be feeling that way, and I knew it, too ... which made me feel even worse. After all, I'd be getting a *bar mitzvah* party next year, and it would be way bigger than Chani's was. We'd have a big catered dinner in a hall, with music and a photographer and everything, and then there would be a *Kiddush* in shul on Shabbos after I leined the *parashah*. And I wouldn't be getting just a few presents. There would be my *tefillin* to buy, and a hat, and a suit. I was starting *bar mitzvah* lessons in just a few weeks, and I usually got excited just thinking about it all.

That night, though, silly as it was, I was feeling jealous of Chani. We'd always shared everything together, fought over everything—and there she was now, sitting up straight and trying to look grown-up in her new Shabbos outfit, smiling at cousins and unwrapping presents. There was no catered dinner, but my mother had spent three nights in the kitchen cooking all of Chani's favorite foods and baking a beautiful cake. The "hall" was our dining room, but you could hardly recognize it with all the balloons and streamers that were hanging from the ceiling.

And me? I hadn't received so much as a "Happy birthday" from anybody. Would it be so terrible, I wondered, if somebody remembered that I'd been born the same time as Chani, even if my *bar mitzvah* wasn't until next year?

Those were the thoughts running through my mind when Zeidy came over to me. He smiled at me, and I could tell that he knew just how I was feeling.

"Happy birthday to my favorite twelve-year-old grandson, Avi," he said, eyes twinkling. Of course, I was the only twelve-year-old grandson at the moment, but Zeidy always manages to make me feel special.

"Thanks, Zeidy!" I said. Maybe I wasn't invisible after all.

That was when Zeidy reached into his pocket and

pulled it out. It looked green and crisp—and suddenly it was in my hand.

"All for you, Avi," said my grandfather. "For a very special birthday boy—on a very special birthday. I think you're old enough to be in charge of your own money now. What do you say?"

I nodded. "Oh, yes, Zeidy! Thank you!" Suddenly, the music seemed exciting and fun again, and my cousins looked eager to play with me. It was as if a dark curtain that had been thrown over the party had been removed. Now I could enjoy it again.

I stuck the money in my pocket and kept it there for the rest of the evening, fingering it every so often. When I went to sleep that night, I placed it on the little table next to my bed.

The twenty-dollar bill was the first thing I saw in the morning, but I hadn't yet decided what to do with it. As I got dressed and ready for school, the possibilities chased through my head, one after the next. I could buy a new CD, or a game. I could save it and see if there was something I really wanted to buy in a few days or weeks or months ….

I put it in the little top drawer of my night table, pressed flat against the right side of the drawer. That's where I always keep my money. Then, as an afterthought, I took it out again and placed it in my shirt pocket. I wanted to take it to school.

That's not a smart idea, a little voice told me. *You'll run around at recess, you'll lose it … and besides, you know what Tatty always says about showing off what you have.*

I discounted the little voice. I'd hide the money in my desk during recess. I'd guard it so carefully, there was no chance anything would happen to it. And I wanted to show it to my friends — Shmully, who always ended up treating me to ice cream because he had money and I didn't, and it was no fun to eat by yourself, and Gedalya, who's about the nicest guy around. I knew he would be as happy with my present as though he'd received it himself. Showing it to my best friends wouldn't be showing off, would it?

I couldn't resist. So I took it to school.

I was as careful with it as I'd told myself I'd be. I couldn't keep myself from sticking my hand into my shirt pocket about once a minute on my way to school, checking to make sure it was still there.

As soon as I got to school, I showed my precious bill to Gedalya and Shmully. Their reactions were just as I'd expected.

"That's great, Avi," Gedalya exclaimed.

"What're you gonna buy with it?" asked Shmully.

"Well, maybe some ice cream first," I answered. "A big

sundae each, okay? Payback for all those times you bailed me out. You too, Gedalya." I was feeling generous, and I could tell that my friends appreciated it. "I dunno about the rest. But I want to get something nice."

"Yeah," Shmully agreed. "It doesn't pay to have a whole twenty and just use it all up on little stuff."

Just then, Yossi walked by. He saw all three of our heads bent over my desk. "What're you guys looking at?" he asked loudly, as he banged into a chair accidentally and sent it crashing to the floor.

"Oh, just something my grandfather gave me for my birthday," I answered, hurriedly shoving the money back into my pocket as Yossi bent down to pick up the chair. Yossi was a great guy, and I didn't care if he knew about my gift, but besides for being extremely clumsy, he also had the loudest voice in the seventh grade. And I didn't really want the whole class to know about my present. That would *really* be showing off.

But it was too late.

"What is it?" he asked again, more loudly still. Heads were starting to turn.

Reluctantly, hoping I could end the scene sooner rather than later, I took out the money and showed it to Yossi. "Just some money."

"Nice!" he bellowed. "A whole twenty! That's great, Avi."

"What did you get twenty dollars for?" asked Yeshaya,

looking a little bit jealous. Everyone knew his family didn't have much money. He'd probably never owned a twenty-dollar bill.

"My birthday," I muttered, shoving it back into my pocket. I suddenly felt really uncomfortable and was relieved when Rabbi Stein walked into the room and everyone went back to their desks.

The little voice in my head started piping up again. *You shouldn't have brought it to school,* it told me. *Look what you did! You made other kids jealous.* Once again, I banished the voice easily to the back of my mind. I hadn't meant for everyone to find out about it, had I? And I was sure they'd all forget about it by recess time.

It seemed like they had forgotten. It was a nice day, and everyone made a beeline for the door. The basketball court was waiting for us. Before I left the room, though, I stuck the twenty-dollar bill into my desk, flat along the right side, just like I did at home. That way, there would be no risk of it falling out during recess.

The game was great but recess was over all too quickly. As soon as I entered the classroom, flushed and breathing hard along with my classmates, I remembered my money. I stuck my hand into the desk.

My twenty-dollar bill was gone.

Gedalya passed my desk on his way to his seat and saw right away that something was wrong. "What's the matter?" he asked.

"My money," I answered through gritted teeth. "It's not here."

"You're sure?" Gedalya bent down and peered into the dark recesses of my desk, which was filled with a hodge-podge of books and notebooks and crumpled papers and empty snack bags and who-knows-what-else.

I was sure. And as I watched Yeshaya walk into the room and look at me sideways, I was suddenly almost certain I knew where my present was.

I never would've thought of Yeshaya as a thief, but I was sure that he'd seen me put away that money at the beginning of recess. He'd *definitely* heard me talking about it; he'd even asked me why I'd been given it. There had been undisguised envy in his eyes then, and he wasn't looking straight at me now. And everyone knew that things were tight in his house.

My first urge was to go talk to Rabbi Stein. I'd tell him that somebody had stolen my money, and who I thought had done it. It had to be done soon, or who knew where Yeshaya would hide it. Then he could just deny having taken it, and nobody would ever be able to find it. So I had to tell my *rebbi* quickly … but for some reason, I didn't.

Rabbi Stein came in and took his seat, and I stayed seated. He began the fifteen-minute *middos shmuess* we have every morning.

The topic was about not embarrassing other people. I

couldn't help staring at my teacher as he talked animatedly. "Embarrassing someone else is like *shefichas damim*—killing him, *chas v'shalom*. Another person's honor and self-respect is worth everything—more than a hundred dollars, or a thousand, or even a million. There are stories about *tzaddikim*—and even about regular Yidden—who were willing to be mocked and blamed and yelled at, just so they wouldn't embarrass another person." Rabbi Stein went on and on, until I realized there was no way I could tell on Yeshaya. Losing twenty dollars—my first twenty-dollar bill ever—was a big thing, but it wasn't as bad as being mocked or blamed or yelled at.

But the money was mine, I argued with myself. Yeshaya had stolen it from me. Wasn't I entitled to try and get it back?

Rabbi Stein had said that preserving another person's honor was more important than all the money in the world. More important than a million dollars. So even if my twenty felt like a million to me right now, it didn't give me the right to embarrass Yeshaya.

That decision couldn't make me like Yeshaya better, though. I spent the whole afternoon wondering what he would do with the money. Would he come to school the next day with a new watch, or a game, or a CD—one that could have been mine?

I wondered whether it was considered embarrassing him if I went over and spoke to him privately. I could go up to Yeshaya during lunch and say, "Look, Yeshaya, I know you took my money. I already decided that I'm not going to tell on you, but you have to give it back to me. Really. It's stealing."

But that would be embarrassing, too. Maybe not as bad as what would happen if I told the *rebbi*, but pretty bad, too.

It was *my* money, though! As much as I thought the matter over, that undisputable fact still came back to me, chasing me in circles. He'd taken my money, and I had a right to get it back. But what did the money mean to me? Would I sell another boy's self-respect for twenty dollars—or a hundred or a thousand or a million? Would I?

The question itself was bigger than twenty dollars. It was a twenty-*thousand*-dollar question!

So I said nothing. Not to Rabbi Stein, not to Yeshaya, and not even to my friends.

That night, I felt silly. What had I been thinking? Rabbi Stein had surely meant not to embarrass somebody in a case where he had a choice to do so or not. I hadn't had a choice! I'd been given a present and it had been my right—no, my responsibility—to tell someone what had happened. Maybe Yeshaya needed help! Maybe …

But deep down, I knew I'd made the right decision. Still, it took me a long time to fall asleep that night.

The next morning, I arrived at school early. I was hoping to search through my desk for the money one more time. Maybe Yeshaya had felt bad. Maybe he'd slipped back into the classroom and returned it.

"Avi?" Someone had walked into the classroom right behind me. The voice was quiet and I couldn't tell who was talking. My first thought was that it must be Yeshaya, coming to apologize.

I turned around. It was Yossi.

My heart fell, even as I slid my hand all along the right side of my desk and felt that there was no crisp money waiting for me.

"Hey, Yossi," I greeted him distractedly. I'd been so hopeful.

"I just wanted to tell you something." Yossi looked very uncomfortable, and I'd never heard him speak so quietly before. "I saw you looking through your desk yesterday and just now, like you lost something …."

"*You* took it?!" I burst out in shock.

Yossi shook his head, hard. "I didn't take anything. I just knocked over your desk yesterday, and everything fell out. It was all over the place. Everyone else had left for recess, so I just stuffed everything back in and ran out. I was embarrassed, and I'm sorry. Are you missing something?"

Maybe … There was a glimmer of hope now. Excitedly, I started rummaging through my desk, sending a cascade of crumpled old papers and empty potato chip bags down to the linoleum floor. And then something else fluttered out.

It was a twenty-dollar bill.

Yossi's eyes widened. "That's what you were missing?"

"Yeah," I answered in wonder.

I put the money back in my pocket, and Yossi helped me carry all the junk over to the garbage can. He knocked the can over once, but I didn't mind. I didn't even make a joke about his clumsiness. I'd just had a real knockout of a lesson on embarrassing people, and I figured Yossi's feelings were worth twenty thousand dollars, too.

The twenty dollars didn't take me as far as I'd thought.

During morning recess, I invited Yossi to join Gedalya, Shmully and me on a trip to the local ice cream shop. He agreed happily. And during afternoon recess, I did something else. I asked Yeshaya to come along, too.

Five ice cream sundaes later, I only had three dollars and change left over. But there were five happy faces and five happy hearts—and mine, I was pretty sure, was the happiest one of all.

My grandparents came to our house for Shabbos that week. "So, Avi," my grandfather asked, "what did you get with your birthday present?"

I thought. "I got a lot of ice cream — and one really big lesson." I knew my grandfather would understand.

"A twenty-dollar lesson?" my grandfather asked with a smile.

"Nah," I answered. "I think maybe more like a twenty-thousand-dollar one."

And after I told my grandfather the whole story, I was pretty sure he felt the same way.

TWO WAYS TO ONE END

Ahuva had been walking for only two minutes, and Mimi's house was clearly in view at the end of the street. They met at the corner midway between the two houses every morning for the walk to school. This corner was now only several hundred yards away, but Mimi was nowhere in sight. Ahuva, however, was not perturbed. The two friends had been meeting at this corner for the past six years, ever since they were in third grade and had received the long-awaited permission to walk to school by themselves.

There were only about twenty sidewalk squares separating Ahuva from the corner when Mimi finally came into view. She emerged from the front door of her house, closed it firmly behind her, and was across her porch, down her front steps and past her lawn in a flash. The squares of sidewalk passed under her feet as if they were the size of dominoes. It wasn't that Mimi ran, because she didn't. She walked, but she walked with a stride so purposeful that it was almost as though the concrete was on fire under her feet.

Ahuva and Mimi met at the corner, as they'd done for six years, at exactly the same time. Ahuva tossed back her long, auburn ponytail and smiled in her laid-back, gentle manner. "Good morning!"

"Good morning!" Mimi responded, tucking a couple of curly, dark brown tendrils firmly behind her ears. Mimi liked everything about her life to be orderly and obedient, and it was a constant source of aggravation that her hair just wouldn't comply. She wasn't out of breath, but her cheeks were flushed from her quick walk down the block.

"So how much cleaning did you get done last night?" Ahuva wasn't curious — she hated cleaning — nor was she competitive, but she knew that Mimi was waiting to be asked.

"Two rooms!" Mimi responded exuberantly. "All by myself. I did my father's study, but that's not too hard since he never really eats in there, and it's mostly *sefarim*. And I cleaned the baby's room. I even found a Cheerio in the closet!" Mimi turned to Ahuva, eyes sparkling.

"Do you have any idea what a good feeling it is to find a real-live, genuine, one-hundred-percent piece of *chametz* when you're cleaning for Pesach? It makes you feel like there's really a point to the cleaning. Sometimes, you can work for hours and hours with no crumbs in sight. There's always dust, of course—but dust isn't *chametz*."

Ahuva nodded. "I know what you mean ... I guess." She smiled. "I can't say I've done too much cleaning so far. Pesach isn't for another couple of weeks. I was supposed to clean my room yesterday, but then Hindy and Avrumy came in and wanted to play a game, so I played with them. And then they wanted to do an arts and crafts project, so we did that, too." She shrugged. "You know, Pesach or not, it's just so nice to be home on a Sunday. I want to spend some of it having a nice time with my family and relaxing—not just working."

Mimi shook her head emphatically. "But Ahuva, the time for relaxing is when the work is *done*, not when there's so much left to do! When the house is clean, you can relax!"

"But then," Ahuva countered gently, "you don't enjoy the time spent preparing for *yom tov*. If you clean everything in a big rush, you miss all the fun of the job."

Anyone watching the two girls arguing could have justifiably felt that this was the first time the difference in opinion had ever come up for discussion. Both faces were earnest; both girls were sure that they were right. And each one was positive that it would only take one more short back-and-forth, one more convincing line, until the other would be won over to her point of view.

But this was no new argument. It was almost a constant disagreement, which came up dozens of times over the course of their friendship. It was pretty much inevitable, considering the differences in opinion between the two girls.

"I mean, Ahuva, what did you get done yesterday? Two shelves? This is the time for action—Pesach is just around the corner! You can't focus on taking the time to *enjoy* the work when there is simply so *much* work to do!" Mimi's voice was animated. She was the doer, the talker, the work-until-you-dropper. But wasn't that the way one should be?

Ahuva continued to smile, and slowly but firmly shook her head. "No, I really feel differently, Mimi. You have to think things out, put feeling into them. You know how we learned that the *chametz* we clean before Pesach is a symbol of the *yetzer hara*. Half the *avodah* of Pesach is thinking about these things and working on ourselves—not just getting things clean. It's important to think things through, to take the time to make other people happy as you go along. Sometimes it's the little things that matter, Mimi—not just getting things done quickly."

"But it's so easy to get sidetracked that way," Mimi protested, gesturing emphatically. "You think that you're just taking the time to help someone or take care of something—and before you know it, you haven't gotten any work done at all! I think that that's the way the *yetzer hara* works!"

Still unruffled, Ahuva shook her head. "It's interesting how we can be such good friends and have such different opinions," she commented.

Mimi's face broke into a smile, too. "True," she agreed.

With that, the argument was dropped as swiftly as it had come up. It was just another battle that had, as usual, ended in a truce with no ground gained on either side. Each girl was sure she was right. And each girl knew that it would take more than another simple argument to win the other over and determine who really was right.

It was a perfect day for Pesach cleaning. That was Mimi's first thought when she opened her eyes on Sunday morning. The sun was shining merrily through her window, and thousands of dancing particles of dust were caught in its rays.

Mimi stretched once and then sprang nimbly out of bed, ready to tackle the day and all the work awaiting her.

It was a perfect day for taking the kids for a trip to the park. That was Ahuva's first thought when she opened her eyes on Sunday morning. The muted clatter coming from the kitchen downstairs told her that her mother had breakfast ready, and was probably already busy with Pesach cleaning.

It would be time for Ahuva to go down soon and help. But it was a Sunday after all … and what was the point of Sunday mornings if you didn't indulge a little? Ahuva took a long, luxurious breath and turned over to catch a few minutes of extra sleep.

Mimi was on her tenth basement shelf and didn't hear her mother enter the room behind her. If she had, she might have been surprised when she looked at her mother. Her mother was gazing at her back and at the neat, dusted shelves with an expression that spoke of something near disapproval.

"Mimi," she said pleasantly after watching her daughter for a few seconds, "I'm going out to do some Pesach shopping with the kids now. Did you have breakfast?"

"Ten shelves!" Mimi told her with satisfaction, turning around for a second to flash a smile and then going right back to the shelf she was dusting. "After this one!"

"And how about a break then, Mimi?" Her mother was concerned. "I don't think you should be working this hard. You need to spend some time outside."

Mimi shrugged. She loved cleaning, the feeling of dust and crumbs and messes melting away under her efficient hands. "That's okay, Ma. I'll finish the shelves first. There are only fifteen left to go, you know."

"If that's what you want, Mimi. But you didn't answer me. Did you have breakfast yet?"

"Yes, I had a cup of orange juice. I didn't have time for anything else yet. Maybe when I finish the shelves ..." Mimi went back to her vigorous dusting.

Her mother left the room, shaking her head slowly back and forth. Mimi certainly didn't seem to mind what she was doing. And if her mother wanted her to learn to go a little slower and be a little less single-minded — well, that just seemed to be something that Mimi would have to do on her own.

"Ahuva, is there any particular cleaning job you'd like to tackle today?" Ahuva's mother asked patiently.

"Oh, nothing in particular," Ahuva answered breezily. "Whatever you tell me. I'll do it as soon as I finish my breakfast. The pancakes are really good, Ma." She took another big bite, followed by a long, leisurely sip of chocolate milk. "Oh, and I told the kids that I'd take them outside today."

"How about cleaning a few living room shelves first?"

"Sure!" Ahuva was agreeable, as always.

Her house had been built at the same time as Mimi's, and it had the same long rows of wooden shelves gracing an entire wall of the living room. Some were filled with *sefarim*, and others were graced by framed pictures and knickknacks.

When Ahuva finished her breakfast, she slowly dragged a stepstool over to the living room shelves and began to dust. The first shelf was filled with pictures. She carefully removed each picture and dusted it before replacing it gently on the shelf. When she was finished, she stopped for a long minute to admire her work and study the smiling faces of her family members. The next shelf contained books.

Ahuva's mother entered the room to find her oldest daughter sitting comfortably on the stepstool and slowly flipping pages of an old book.

"Ahuva?"

"Ma, I haven't read this in ages!" Ahuva looked up, eyes shining. "I had no idea we still had it! Don't you love this book?"

Ahuva's mother stifled a sigh. "Ahuva, why don't you put it aside to read when you're finished with the shelves?"

"Oh, sure." Ahuva put it down on the end table and continued dusting while she hummed, scanned titles and flipped through pages to find fondly remembered favorite scenes.

During her mother's next visit to the room, she found Ahuva turning the pages of an old photo album, a small smile on her face.

"Ahuva?" she said.

"Yes? Oh sorry, Ma." Ahuva put down the book and resumed dusting. "I just saw that old photo album; it has such cute pictures of when the twins were babies …."

"Ahuva, why don't you finish the shelf and take the kids out to play?" her mother asked, resigned. It was the best job for Ahuva, really. She had endless patience for both shelves and children, but … well, the shelves didn't really need or appreciate her loving care.

"Great! No problem, Ma!" Ahuva went on dusting in her slow, careful way — just the tiniest bit more quickly now that she had the outing to the park to look forward to.

It was the first day of the pre-Pesach day camp, and as far as the two young counselors were concerned, the day was turning out to be a smashing success. They'd already produced a Pesach-themed craft project, eaten a snack and visited the playground. Now they were back in their basement room for lunch and a few quiet games and stories before it would be time for the parents to pick them up.

It was when Shoshie closed the basement door behind her that the trouble started. "Not seven, not eight, not nine …" She counted heads. "Nine?" She turned to Chaya, the other counselor, in alarm. "But we had ten, didn't we?"

Chaya's face mirrored her dismay. "Of course there were ten!" She repeated the counting, just to be sure. There were still only nine. "Who's missing?" she asked desperately.

"Rochy's here, Michoel's here, Toby's here … Where's Yitzy?"

He wasn't in the room.

"He was with us at the park," Chaya remembered. "I remember watching him go down the big slide."

"You stay here," Shoshie said frantically. "I'll run back to the playground. He's got to still be there, right?" She flew out the door.

Little Yitzy, with his soulful brown eyes and blond pigtails, was nowhere to be found. "Yitzy!" Shoshie shouted. "Yitzy! Where are you?" Heads turned and mothers stared, but no little blond head peeped out at her from behind the playground equipment.

Tears sprang to Shoshie's eyes. She'd been babysitting for years, and everyone said that she was so caring and responsible. How had this happened? And where was Yitzy? Her heart pounded desperately inside her chest. Was he scared? Hurt? Was he trying to cross a busy street by himself at this very moment?

"Yitzy!" she cried again, urgently. There was no answer.

Mimi was deep in the middle of a shelf when she heard noise coming from the front porch of her house. It sounded like footsteps — small, pattering ones. She frowned. Her youngest sibling was five-year-old Tully. This sounded like a younger kid. Unless it was a squirrel. She shrugged. It didn't really matter. Neighbors were always coming over. If somebody wanted something, she'd hear a knock on the door.

The footsteps stopped, and Mimi went on dusting. She only had another eight shelves to go … She frowned. Maybe it was a little kid out there, not a squirrel … and maybe the kid needed help. Maybe it wasn't someone she knew. Maybe he or she was too shy to knock on the door.

With a sigh of resignation, Mimi put down her dust

rag and hopped off the stepstool. She walked across the living room to the front door and opened it wide.

"Hey!" she said, surprised. There was a little boy standing on her porch. He looked so woebegone that Mimi thought she'd never seen a sorrier face. "What is your name?"

The little boy just burst into tears. Mimi cast a regretful look toward the shelves. *Oh, well. So much for getting the shelves done.* She sat down on the steps next to him, reached for his hand and purposefully lowered her voice. "Come, sit down with me."

The little boy didn't say anything but he sat down, still sobbing. Mimi stared down at the little charge she found herself saddled with, just when she was making real headway on the shelves. She quickly ran inside and fetched a lollypop for him from the nosh cabinet, which he accepted. His tears abated somewhat. She thought about helping him find his family, but she had no idea where he'd come from, so where was she supposed to return him? She also considered bringing him inside, settling him on a chair with his lollypop, and going back to the shelves ….

But something about his sad little face made her push the shelves out of her mind for a minute. Something Ahuva had said popped into her head.

It's important to think things through, to take the time to make other people happy as you go along. Sometimes it's the little things that matter, Mimi—not just getting things done quickly.

What could she do to make this little kid happy? Mimi bent down until she was at eye level. "What's your name?" she said again, softly.

This time, Yitzy managed to answer—but the answer was so tangled up with the lollypop in his mouth that Mimi couldn't make out a syllable. It was only on the third try—with the lollypop reluctantly removed—that she caught the name.

"Okay, Yitzy, let me make a few calls. I'm going to try to find your family, okay?" Yitzy, of course, had very little idea of what Mimi was saying, but the gently reassuring note in her voice calmed him, and he sat quietly while Mimi quickly fetched the phone.

Mimi called several friends and neighbors who had two-year-olds at home. Nobody knew of a little blond Yitzy. Everyone promised to make a couple of calls to see if they could track down the little boy's parents.

After the last call, Mimi put the phone down slowly. She'd done what she could. Now all she could do was wait. Surely she could go back to the shelves now, couldn't she?

She found that she couldn't. Not with Yitzy's big, trusting brown eyes staring up at her. She remembered what Ahuva had said about making other people happy, doing little things for others—not just getting things done. The shelves would wait.

"Want me to read you a book?" she asked.

When Mimi's mother arrived home from shopping, her jaw dropped. Mimi was seated on the front steps, a picture book wide open on her lap. A little boy with blond pigtails leaned against her, a lollypop in his mouth and deep brown eyes glued to Mimi's face. The strangest thing about the whole picture was the serene, peaceful expression on Mimi's face.

"Yitzy!"

The desperation in the caller's voice pulled Ahuva out of her happy bubble. She gave her little brother's swing one more push and turned to locate the source of the call. Almost immediately she spotted a girl, just a couple of years younger than herself, standing in the middle of the playground and looking around wildly.

"Push me, Ahuva!" Meir called.

"Wait a minute," Ahuva answered. She raised her voice. "Do you need help with something?" she addressed the girl standing and scanning the park equipment.

"I lost a kid! Someone I was babysitting for, and he's only two years old! He was just here a few minutes ago, and we haven't seen him since."

Ahuva's face showed the sympathy she felt for the worried girl. She wanted to reassure her, to help out ...

but what could she do? The kid wasn't here. For a second, she imagined the way the younger girl must feel, and how the little lost boy must feel. Where could he be?

Suddenly, she remembered the conversation that she'd had with Mimi almost a week ago. Mimi had talked about taking the initiative, about getting things done.

Well, now was the time to put thoughts aside and take action. The younger girl was clearly too distraught to think clearly, but Ahuva wasn't used to making decisions and carrying them out either ….

"Um," she said. "I guess we'd better look for him." As her thoughts crystallized to form a solid plan, she began to speak more clearly and confidently. "You go down the block that way and look." She pointed. "Look around houses and in bushes, too, and knock on doors. See if anyone's seen him. I'll go the other way with my brother and sister and look. We'll meet back here in twenty minutes to report."

Exactly ten minutes later, Ahuva found herself standing on Mimi's porch. "Hi, Mimi," she said. "Have you seen a— Hey, is that him?"

"Are you looking for Yitzy?" Mimi asked with a smile.

"Yes! There was a girl watching him in the park and he got lost somehow. We've been scouring the street looking for him. The girl's a wreck; I'd better get right back to her and let her know that Yitzy's been found." Ahuva spoke uncharacteristically rapidly.

In just seconds, the two friends had parted ways. Neither of them knew it, but they'd each carried away a little of the other as a result of that afternoon's events.

"Mimi, it's my turn to squirt!" Mimi passed the squeeze bottle to her little brother. Who said cleaning the chairs couldn't be done with a younger sibling? She ducked to avoid the fine stream of water directed right at her face. It would take a lot longer this way, but wasn't having fun half the point?

"The shelves are half done," Ahuva reported to her mother, as she slid into her seat for supper.

Her mother looked up, startled. "Really? When did you do that?"

"Oh, just now. In the last hour and a half. I just buckled down and got to work." Ahuva grinned. "I don't know what came over me, but it feels good."

"You know how we were discussing Pesach cleaning last week?" Mimi asked as she met Ahuva at the corner the next morning.

Ahuva nodded.

"Well, I was thinking you were right—sometimes. About taking your time and paying attention to people while you work …"

"That's funny," Ahuva said slowly, "because I was thinking you're right, too—sometimes. Sometimes you have to just focus and get things done."

"Maybe," Mimi commented reflectively, "in different situations, there are different ways to reach one goal. Different means to an end, you know? And you just have to pick the right one. I think that's the hard part."

As the two girls fell into step together, they thought about the brand-new lesson they had just learned—about work and discipline, love and caring—and how to put all the pieces together to accomplish an important goal.

COUNTDOWN

The atmosphere in the classroom was grim. Most of the girls in the room were crowded around Hadassah's desk.

"Are you sure?" Malya asked.

Hadassah nodded self-importantly. "Absolutely. My aunt is the assistant principal. If she says that Mrs. Rotkin is staying for another month, then that means she's staying for another month."

"A whole *month*!" Rivky exclaimed.

"That's a long time," Sara agreed.

A cloak of mournfulness descended over the group.

Esther was the one to break the silence. "Well, look at the bright side," she said. "Mrs. Rotkin is probably just as unhappy as we are with the arrangements."

Her classmates went on the attack. "What do you mean, as unhappy as we are?" demanded Sara. "She *wanted* this job, didn't she? She applied for it!"

"She accepted it," Shaindy seconded.

"And we were supposed to get Mrs. Ellis," Malya concluded sadly.

Esther spoke up again. "It's not Mrs. Rotkin's fault that we didn't get Mrs. Ellis."

Vivi came to Esther's defense. "She's just doing her job. She's probably a good teacher, if we would just give her a—"

But Vivi's sentence was cut short by her classmates.

"How can you say that?"

"She's sent almost everyone in our class to the principal at least once! And she's only been here six weeks!"

"Well, think about how our class has been behaving," Vivi retorted. "It's not like we've been giving Mrs. Rotkin an easy time …"

"Well, what about those hard quizzes? *Those* aren't her fault?"

"And the homework! Much more than we ever had before! Why does she give so much work?"

Vivi just closed her mouth. She looked at Esther, who simply shrugged. *They're not going to listen to us anyway,* her eyes said. *Maybe we should just stop arguing.*

Malya followed the unspoken conversation between the two friends and felt a pang. She thought about how her teacher must feel—the way any teacher would feel about being asked to substitute for the school's most popular eighth-grade teacher on such short notice, the way she herself would feel about walking into a classroom full of hostile, disappointed girls who were determined to test her in every way their active thirteen-year-old minds could dream up—but her thoughts were quickly drowned out by the cacophony of shouts swirling around her.

Eventually, the hubbub died down as girls began returning to their desks and taking out their lunches. It *was* lunchtime, after all. Mrs. Rotkin wasn't due back in the classroom for another twenty minutes or so.

Malya had a sunny personality, and she'd only taken two bites of her sandwich before she had something positive to share. "At least we'll have Mrs. Ellis back in a month."

"Who says she'll come back then?" Rochel challenged. "She was supposed to come back next week, and now they're saying that she's taking off even more time to spend with her baby."

"Another whole month is a long time," Sara said.

"Well, we'll enjoy the rest of the year even more after this," Malya interjected.

"Yeah," said Shira, trying to assume a positive point of view. "And it's really just four weeks."

"There are five school days in every week," Shaindy said slowly. "So that's only twenty more days."

"Let's make a countdown!" Mindy exclaimed.

"Yes!" Dena, always one for action, jumped into high gear and hurried up to the blackboard. She grabbed a thick piece of chalk. "TWENTY DAYS LEFT," she wrote out carefully in huge block letters.

"You'd better erase that," Esther warned. "We'll all get in trouble, and besides, it's really not nice."

Rochel shrugged. "You really think anyone will know what we're talking about?"

"Is it worth the chance?" Rivky said worriedly.

"I'm telling you, you better take it off," Esther said. "We really, really don't want Mrs. Rotkin to walk in and see that."

"Why not?" Shaindy asked, with a toss of her long blond ponytail. "Maybe then she'd have an idea of how unhappy we are."

Everyone knew it wasn't a serious suggestion, but Esther and Vivi were about to speak up anyway.

Before they could, though, Dena suggested, "Let's make it better." She grabbed the chalk once more and wrote the words "GOOD-BYE, MRS. ROTKIN!" in even bigger letters underneath the ones already adorning the board.

By now, even some of the girls who were very unhappy with Mrs. Rotkin felt uncomfortable about the words Dena had written on the board. It was one thing to complain about a teacher, and another thing entirely to be openly counting down the days remaining until her departure.

"Erase it now," Kaila insisted.

"What's the rush? There's five more minutes left to lunch," Dena argued.

"Actually, this is healthy," Shaindy said pompously. "It's allowing us to express our pain and frustration."

Several classmates cackled with laughter. "And who made you such an expert?" Rochel demanded.

"My aunt's a social worker," Shaindy answered in her loftiest manner. "She was at our house for Shabbos and told us—"

Nobody ever discovered what Shaindy's aunt had told her, because just then the door swung open and—

Mrs. Rotkin walked into the room.

"Girls, I wanted to explain something about the homework," Mrs. Rotkin began. Her students never found out that extra information, because Mrs. Rotkin noticed that some of the girls seemed to be almost in shock, and others were staring behind her at the blackboard.

Malya felt as if her mind was frozen. She helplessly willed her classmates to look away from the board and act naturally, but she knew it was too late. Mrs. Rotkin might be a tough teacher, but she sure wasn't stupid. If half the class was staring at the blackboard, she was going to turn around and look at it, too.

She did. Malya wished she could hide under her desk

or leave the room, as she stared in horrified fascination at Mrs. Rotkin's back while the teacher stood there, staring at the blackboard for what seemed an inordinately long time. The seconds stretched into minutes. Malya thought that she had never heard the classroom so quiet. She could hear the soft humming of the fluorescent lights, and even the breathing of the girl next to her.

After what seemed an eternity, Mrs. Rotkin turned around and left the room. Just like that. She didn't say anything, and she didn't even glance in their direction.

"We shouldn't have done that," Vivi squeaked.

Esther just groaned.

"Oh, boy, are we going to get in trouble," Mindy muttered under her breath.

"You think she'll go to the principal?" Rochel asked worriedly, pushing her bangs out of her eyes the way she always did when she was nervous.

"I think we can count on that," Hadassah concluded gloomily.

"You shouldn't have written that terrible thing," Tova told Dena, arms crossed.

"What?!" Dena whirled on Tova. "It was *not* my idea!" As if to underscore that fact, she hurried up to the board and began to erase the offending words.

"It was just a joke," Mindy, who had suggested the countdown in the first place, protested weakly. "I didn't mean that you should really—"

It was Esther who spoke up loudly. "It's everybody's fault, okay?"

"Except for you and Vivi, you mean?" Shaindy asked cynically.

"No, even us. Because we should have tried harder to stop you," Esther replied.

Malya stared down at her desk. It was her fault, too, she thought. She'd known this was wrong from the start. She could have protested along with Esther and Vivi. But she'd been sent to the principal herself last week, so she'd had mixed feelings toward Mrs. Rotkin.

The eighth graders sat on pins and needles all day, waiting for the principal to march into the room.

At three-thirty, Malya turned around in her seat to face Sara. "There's only one more hour left," she whispered. "It looks like the principal isn't coming."

Sara shook her head. "Don't be so sure," she whispered.

But the principal didn't come into their classroom that day. When the final bell rang and the girls hurried to pack up their things and get ready to leave, the feeling of relief in the room was palpable.

"The principal never came," Rochel whispered.

"But what about tomorrow?" Malya asked.

Sara nodded. "What are we going to do when Mrs. Rotkin comes in, even if the principal isn't with her?"

No one answered. They weren't looking forward to seeing Mrs. Rotkin the next day. How do you act normally in front of a person who knows without a shadow of a doubt that you're counting the days until she leaves?

The moment arrived all too soon. For once, all of the girls were in their seats, ready and waiting quietly for the bell to ring.

Mrs. Rotkin walked in right on time. Her face was so hard and cold, it looked as if someone had carved it from stone and put it on display in the classroom. *Compared to the way she looks now,* Malya thought, *Mrs. Rotkin seemed downright friendly and good-natured before.* There was nothing friendly or good-natured about the expression on her face just then. And that, Malya couldn't help thinking, was all their fault.

No one passed notes or whispered or called out in class that morning. The first time Mrs. Rotkin asked for a volunteer to read a *Rashi*, Malya was startled to find her own hand up in the air—and even more surprised when she realized it was not alone. Esther and Vivi had their hands raised, of course, but there were another half dozen waving in the air, as though Mrs. Rotkin was their favorite teacher and they'd all prepared the night before for the lesson, the way they were supposed to.

Except that … it seemed that everyone *had* prepared the night before. Malya realized that as soon as Rochel started to read. She said the words clearly, paused in the right places and promptly answered Mrs. Rotkin's question on the meaning of a difficult word.

Why am I surprised? Malya asked herself. After all, she had also prepared for class.

By the end of the class, Mrs. Rotkin's expression looked different. At least, that was the consensus of her students at a hurried conference held during lunchtime.

"She doesn't look as mad anymore," Shaindy whispered.

"You're right …" Hadassah said thoughtfully.

"You know what?" said Malya, before she could help it. "Her lesson was pretty good today, wasn't it?"

Esther sighed. "Her lessons are always good, but you guys are too busy with your own stuff to notice."

"That doesn't make sense," Dena argued. "We wouldn't have been busy with our own stuff if the lessons had been interesting."

Malya took a deep breath and shook her head. "I don't think so. I think we were all just so upset about not having Mrs. Ellis that we kind of … got carried away."

"We never gave her a chance," Rivky agreed.

"Do you think the principal will come in today?" Mindy asked nervously, changing the subject.

"Nah," said Hadassah. "If she didn't talk to us yesterday — or this morning — then Mrs. Rotkin probably didn't tell her what happened."

"Maybe," Rivky said ominously, "she has something much, much worse in store for us."

"Worse?" Vivi asked blankly. "What's worse than going to the principal?"

"Yeah," Sara said. "I mean, we're eighth graders in Bais Yaakov. She can't exactly send us off to the torture chambers or something like that."

"Even if she wanted to," Dena giggled. "Good luck finding a good, old-fashioned torture chamber in this neighborhood."

"Maybe she'll call in the administrator," Shaindy suggested.

"Rabbi Reiner? Nah, why would she do that? He's too nice. He wouldn't punish us."

The bell rang, the conversation ended and the girls went back to their classroom. But throughout the afternoon they watched the door nervously, just in case the principal did walk in.

After that, school continued as usual, but it was a different class than the one that had been there during the first few months of the year. The girls were prepared for class. They were polite and respectful. They never spoke out of turn—until one day, a few weeks after the fateful blackboard incident.

The *parashah* class that week had led into a lesson on honesty. "Are there times," Mrs. Rotkin asked, "when people do things that seem honest, but really are motivated by dishonesty? Or times when people do things that on the surface appear dishonest, but are really done for the right reasons?"

The girls processed the questions, and then hands started to go up. These weren't the perfunctory, be-polite-to-Mrs.-Rotkin hands that had gone up a couple of weeks ago. The hands were eager, sticking straight up in the air, waving wildly.

"Yes, Shaindy?"

Shaindy had an example, and then Dena had an opinion, which Hadassah agreed with. Soon there were no hands being raised, just voices calling out and arguing heatedly, laughing, debating ….

Mrs. Rotkin was at the center of it all, making sure all the girls got their turn to speak, agreeing with some comments and taking issue with others. It was such a good class that nobody had time to analyze what had happened — until later.

During lunch, Malya turned to Sara. "That was an awesome class, wasn't it?"

"Yeah," Sara said. "I loved the way she kept giving examples."

"And she let us participate," Dena said. "That's the only way I can pay attention."

"You know what?" Rivky said thoughtfully. "This is the way I thought class would be with Mrs. Ellis. I don't think she could be that much better than Mrs. Rotkin is now."

Hadassah sighed. "It's really too bad that we were so mean to her at the beginning of the year."

"Yeah," Esther agreed sadly.

Malya admired Esther's self-control in not telling them all "I told you so."

"Do you think she even knows that we love her classes?" Rochel asked.

"I doubt it," Hadassah said. "I mean, she knows we're not bad in class anymore, but maybe she thinks it's because we feel guilty."

"It's too bad we can't let her know," Miri murmured.

Malya sat straight up, eyes sparkling. "Who says we can't?"

"What're you going to do — write a letter?" Hadassah asked skeptically.

"Not exactly," Malya responded. "Why not let her know the same way we did last time?"

Everyone looked at her, confused.

"Huh?" Shaindy asked. "We never let her know …"

"I get it!" Dena exclaimed suddenly. She ran up to the blackboard and grabbed the chalk. On the board, in huge bold letters, she wrote "MRS. ROTKIN IS THE GREATEST!"

"Good enough?" asked Malya, turning to the class.

It was eerily similar to that other afternoon, weeks earlier.

Then, before anyone could answer, Mrs. Rotkin

walked in. "Girls," she said. "I wanted to let you know about the quiz next week, so you can start —" She stopped mid-sentence, as she saw everyone staring over her shoulder ... once again.

The smile on her face disappeared. She did not turn around. "— so that you can start studying," she finished. "It will be on the last two *perakim* we covered — *Chumash* and *Rashi*. Read through your notes and you should do fine."

Then she quickly turned to leave the room.

"Uh, Mrs. Rotkin?" Shaindy called out timidly. "Aren't you going to look at the blackboard?"

Mrs. Rotkin stared at the class for a long moment, and then turned to the board. This time, it seemed as if she'd stand there forever. But when she turned around, it was with a big smile on her face. And somehow, the girls knew that this was the way they'd always remember her — smiling at the front of the room, with all of them sitting around and smiling back.

GLOSSARY

*All terms are Hebrew unless indicated
as Yiddish (Yidd.) or Aramaic (Aram.).*

Avodah — service

Baal chessed — one who excels at acts of kindness

Bar mitzvah — age thirteen, when a Jewish male becomes obligated to observe the Torah commandments

Baruch Hashem — thank the Almighty

Bas mitzvah — age twelve, when a Jewish female becomes obligated to observe the Torah commandments

Bentcher *(Yidd.)* — booklet containing the Grace after Meals prayer

Brachah — blessing

Bubby *(Yidd.)* — grandmother

Challah — traditional bread used on the Sabbath and holidays

Chametz — leavened bread, which is forbidden on Passover

Chanukah — holiday that celebrates the victory of the Chashmona'im over the Syrian Greeks during the era of the Second Temple

Chas v'shalom — Heaven forbid

Chasunah — wedding

Chavrusa *(Aram.)* — Torah study partner

Chessed — kindness

Chumash — the Five Books of Moses

Chutzpah *(Yidd.)* — brazenness

Chutzpahdik *(Yidd.)* — brazen

Daven, davening *(Yidd.)* — pray, praying

Eretz Yisrael — the Land of Israel

Erev — lit., "the eve of"; the day before

Frum *(Yidd.)* — religiously observant

Gelt *(Yidd.)* — money

Halachah, halachos — Jewish law(s)

Hashavas aveidah — returning a lost object

Hashem — the Almighty

Hasmadah — diligence

Hechsher — stamp of kosher certification

Kehillah — congregation

Kiddush — blessing that sanctifies the Sabbath or holiday; also, the reception that sometimes follows the Sabbath morning prayers

Lashon hara — gossip

Lein, leined *(Yidd.)* — chant(ed) the weekly Torah portion from the Torah scroll

Maariv — evening prayers

Machanayim — a ball game

Makpid — particular

Mazel tov — good luck

Menorah — candelabra used on Chanukah

Middah, middos—character trait(s)

Milchig *(Yidd.)*—dairy

Minchah—afternoon prayers

Mishnah Berurah—classic work of Jewish law

Mitzvah, mitzvos—Torah commandment(s)

Motzaei—the night following

Mussar—rebuke

Navi—the books of the Prophets

Oy, vey *(Yidd.)*—oh, woe

P'shetel *(Yidd.)*—speech given by a *bar mitzvah* boy

Parashah—weekly Torah portion

Pareve *(Yidd.)*—neither dairy nor meat

Perakim—chapters

Pesach—Passover, which celebrates Hashem's redemption of the Jews from slavery in Egypt

Rashi—classic Torah commentator

Rebbi, rebbeim—Torah teacher(s)

Refuah sheleimah—a full recovery

Rosh Hashanah—the Jewish New Year

Sefer, sefarim—Torah book(s)

Seichel—intelligence

Shabbos—Sabbath

Shefichas damim—murder

Shema—fundamental Jewish prayer that declares the unity of the Almighty

Shmuess *(Yidd.)*—discourse, talk

Shul *(Yidd.)* — synagogue

Siman — a definitive sign

Simchah — happy occasion

Siyum — celebration on completing the study of a major Torah work

Sukkah — temporary dwelling used on the holiday of Sukkos

Sukkos — the holiday of Tabernacles

Tafkid — purpose

Tante *(Yidd.)* — aunt

Tatty *(Yidd.)* — father

Tefillin — phylacteries; black boxes containing scrolls with certain Torah portions, worn by adult Jewish men during morning prayers

Tzaddikim — righteous people

Tzedakah — charity

Yamim Nora'im — the High Holy Days

Yarmulke *(Yidd.)* — skullcap

Yeshivah — Torah school

Yetzer hara — the evil inclination

Yidden *(Yidd.)* — Jews

Yiddishkeit *(Yidd.)* — Judaism

Yom Kippur — the Day of Atonement

Yom Tov, Yamim Tovim — holiday(s)

Zeidy *(Yidd.)* — grandfather